LORD, I CAN'T KEEP LIVIN' LIKE THIS!

The story of a young man trying to find redemption on the cruel and cold-hearted streets of Southern California.

A.J. Scott

ISBN: 978-0-9832501-0-4
LCCN: 2011960823

Published by:
Muse Publication
2127 Olympic Parkway Suite 1006, #234 Chula Vista, CA. 91915
Editorial Services & Formatting provided By: Cris Wanzer/Manuscripts To Go
Cover Art Donated by: Gregory De`Quon Caruth

Tell us what you think about our story. Or, if you would like more information about the author or what inspired this book, please write to: musepublication.com

Printed in the United States of America

This book is dedicated to my mother, who has been a beacon of inspiration in my life.

Foreword

I am very elated by the fact that Amos Scott is a changed man, redeemed by the Blood of Jesus Christ. The Bible says in Galatians 3:13, "Christ has redeemed us from the curse of the law, being made a curse for us: for it is written, cursed is every one that hangs on a tree." My emphasis here is on the word "redeemed." Meaning that Christ has purchased us for Himself with His own Blood. Therefore, Amos Scott, as well as all born-again people, belong to Jesus Christ and Him alone.

I have known Amos Scott for quite a few years. He was once a member of the church that I pastor. Even at that time I could see that God had a useful purpose for his life. Even though he has gone through much, the purpose of God in his life is being lived out. Personally, I see Amos as a wonderful, talented, respectful, and bright young man who is a useful servant in the hands of God. To me, that's wonderful.

Many authors are able to put into narrative form the experiences that they have had in life. These experiences can be either personal or experiences as witnessed in the communities in which they have lived. Amos Scott has done a wonderful job in the setting and narration of this life-changing book. This book takes one into the very life of the streets, the hoods of Southern California, prison, and freedom. However, the lessons to be learned from reading this book could very well be learned in any urban city in America, and perhaps the world. Hopefully, many young as well as older people will, after *reading LORD, I Can't Keep Living Like This!,* perhaps identify with the many negative areas of life, desire a change, and attain one.

I am grateful that God has put such a book into the heart of Amos Scott. In reading this book, my eyes were opened to many things that even I, as a minister of the gospel have not been familiar with. I gained a greater understanding of life that is happening around me at any given time. It showed me the struggles that many people wrestle with. I understand that many die, yet there are those who seemingly are held by the purpose of God.

I feel that many young people will be changed by reading this book. They will understand that God has created a better life for them that is attainable, among many other great things.

I pray blessings upon this book and every person that reads it. Not only the readers, also everyone that the readers are connected to, in the Name of Jesus Christ, Our Wonderful Savior.

— Pastor Robert E. Funchess, Ph.D.

Acknowledgments

GOD HAS HIS WAY of placing certain people in our life's pathway to assist and inspire us. I cannot possibly start to thank everyone who listened and gave their undivided attention and advice while I was writing this book, yet there are five people who come to mind. Thanks to…

My mother, Bessie L. Scott, for your continuous prayers and support. I wouldn't have the faith I have today without first witnessing what God has done in your life.

Antonine Robinson, my friend, brother and dawg, for his much needed assistance, guidance and patience while staying awake many late nights to help me prepare the foundation of this book. Twan, God has made room for your gift, as well.

My friend Ralph Thompson, for the advice, and many hours you've run by my side and listened to me ramble as we jogged our lives away. Thank you for your patience and prayers. I ran eleven miles today!

My muse, this task would have been impossible without you. Thank you for your inspiration, understanding, and guidance.

The reader, I thank you for the time you've taken to open and read this book. I pray the message will inspire and become a blessing to you as much as it has been a blessing to me.

Thank you all.

Contents

Chapter One

The 'hood was about as calm as any gang-infested neighborhood in Southern California could be. Gang-bangers young and old hung out on street corners, selling drugs, smoking weed, shooting dice and playing loud music by DJ. Khalid and T. Pain. They all sang along with the lyrics. "All I do is win, win, win, no matter what," came blaring from car speakers as they waved their hands in the air.

The sight of little kids running around playing with super soakers and water hoses marked an approaching summer that would find all those men and women enjoying themselves in California's sun. In other words, it was a typical afternoon.

Ray was a young, African-American man. He had just come out of a backyard wearing a pair of green Dickies that slightly sagged below his waist, a white T-shirt with a wife beater underneath, and a pair of Air Force Ones that matched his shirt. His slim, five-foot-ten frame complemented his freshly done, French braided hair that hung past his shoulders. As he took a look around in both directions, he heard someone yell his name from across the street. One glance and he immediately knew who it was.

That Skeeza' Ketta, he thought. "Girl, what you want?" he hollered back to her.

Ketta was a neighborhood junkie Ray had known most of his life. But from the day she got old man Jesse drunk, cut off his pockets with a razor blade, and robbed him of his Social Security check he'd just received, she was known for being scandalous and up to no good. She'd looked good in her day. With her caramel brown complexion and curvaceous body, she'd resembled a young Whitney Houston. But now, after letting herself go to drug addiction, she would do good to be in the same category as

Amy Winehouse, at best.

Ray shook his head in disbelief as he met the woman whose tattered, cut off jeans, halter top and broken sandal straps made her to look as if she had never known what a good shower and clean clothes felt like. It was hard to believe that a few years back she had been a highly regarded school teacher, married, with two beautiful children.

"L'il Ray," she said through tarnished teeth. "You gotta twenty?" She asked this even though she knew that Ray had drugs on him at all times.

Ray shook his head in disbelief. "Why, do you have twenty dollars?"

The woman shuffled her feet and rocked from side to side with a pleading look in her eyes. "L'il Ray, you know me, baby. Don't play any games. If you let me get one until later, I'll have your money."

"Ketta, you still owe me the twenty I gave you last week when you came to the spot in that car. You said you needed to show it to someone and never came back."

"But..." Ketta interjected, but was cut off.

"But nothin'. I'm not givin' you nothin' until you pay me first. You need to get yourself together anyway, walkin' around here lookin' like death."

"Ain't that the kettle callin' the pot black?" Ketta mumbled underneath her breath.

Ray paused. "What you say?"

She sighed. "Nothin', nothin'," she 'fessed up. "L'il Ray, baby, stop trippin'. Man you can trust me just this one time, baby?"

"Trust..." Ray started, but was instantly cut off by the persistent woman.

"Yeah, trust. After today I'm through with this stuff anyways. I'mma start goin' to church or somethin' because I'm tired of livin' like this. So, come on, baby," she begged.

"Like I was about to say," Ray responded. "In the

streets, we ain't supposed to trust nobody. But what I will do is make you a deal."

"What kind of deal?" she asked, placing her hands on her hips. "Ray, you know I ain't..."

"Man, naw! I ain't talkin' about tryin' to do nothin' with you," he interjected in awe. "What I was about to say is, if you go to church, we'll squash that twenty. Because girl, I know you ain't goin' nowhere near a church!" Then Ray turned and walked away, as Ketta exhaled heavily, stomped her feet, and clenched her fists tightly together.

This was Magnolia Street, Ray's neighborhood, on the west side of San Bernardino. It was its own little world, surrounded by other neighborhoods that made up that side of town. It was rare that Ray left the area because anything and everything he needed was right there.

Ray noticed a light grey 1984 Cutlass coming up the street as he began to walk across it. Instantly, he recognized that it was his homeboy, Casper, from the projects. Stopping to wait for his partner, Ray wanted to see what he was up to. Pulling up on Ray's side, Casper leaned out of his window, showcasing an all-white, fitted baseball cap that had "Westside" embroidered across the front in Old English lettering.

"What's up, dawg?" Ray asked as they gave each other some dap. "Where's the money at?"

Casper looked at his young friend and smiled. His red hair and albino pigmentation made him stand out compared to the rest of his family. "You tell me, baller. They say you and Big Mack is doin' big things around here."

"Naw, they lyin'," Ray replied. "Don't believe everything you hear. Ya' boy out here thirsty!"

The bass that shook from Casper's trunk made it hard for Ray to hear him. "I saw a few cats down on Flores Street shootin' dice," Casper told him. "It looks like it's gettin' crazy over there," Casper smiled. He knew Ray loved to shoot craps, and it showed in his eyes.

"Is that right?"

"Yeah, I was gonna stop, but I gotta pick up my baby momma from her mom's spot."

Ray bobbed his head. "I just might go down there and break them suckas," he said with confidence.

Casper laughed, and then as an afterthought said, "Oh yeah! Don't you got that fool Upshaw as your probation officer?"

Just the mention of Upshaw's name put Ray on alert. "Yeah, why, what's up?"

Casper turned his music down before he spoke. "You know, I got that fool too. He just pulled up on me at Muscoy Liquor. At first I didn't know it was him. You know, that fool is crazy."

Crazy isn't the word. Upshaw is burnt out! Ray thought. "So, what happened?" he asked.

"Man, that fool pulled up in a 'Lac on some True Spokes and white walls."

"True Spokes!"

"Yeah! You know, I thought it looked crazy 'cause cats ain't rolled Trues since the eighties. But when I looked, it's this fool, lookin' like some type of OG or somethin'."

Ray couldn't help but laugh to himself. Officer Upshaw had been his probation officer for the past year and a half. He hadn't reported to him in a few months and Ray knew that nine times out of ten, Upshaw was looking for him. He really wasn't in the mood for seeing Upshaw because when he did, Ray always had a feeling he was going to get locked up.

"So, what he say?" Ray asked Casper.

"Well, I had just reported last week so he didn't say nothin' but 'What's up?' I told him nothin' and went into the store. When I came out this fool was posted up on the wall like he was servin' or somethin'. Smoked out Nate, even pushed up on him and asked him for a twenty. I almost died!"

Ray couldn't believe what he was hearing.

"I mean," Casper continued, "he's up there right now. This fool got an Adidas suit on. One of those tight track suits from the eighties with a leather godfather hat and a thick gold rope around his neck. He looked like a white out-of-date rapper who was dressed like Run-DMC."

Ray started laughing when he pictured officer Upshaw dressed like that. "What did he say when Nate asked for the twenty?"

"This fool told him that he was out and he had to re-up. Nate didn't even know that he was the police!"

That was just like Nate. He was so smoked out that he would buy drugs from anybody. Thinking fast, Ray asked, "How long ago was this?"

"Just now," Casper told him. "I'm tellin' you, that fool is probably still up there."

"Good lookin' out," Ray told his friend. "That fool might wanna slide through here."

"What? Is he lookin' for you?"

Probably, Ray thought. Ray didn't plan on taking any risks, so he said his farewells to his friend, and made his way down to Flores Street. That way, he could see what was up with that dice game while keeping an eye out for that crazy P.O. of his. *Yeah,* Ray thought, *typical day in the 'hood.*

Chapter Two

It was a hot summer day on the streets of Southern California. The weather was perfect for all the players who had low riders to showcase their toys. Big Mack parked his Black Raven 2009 Cadillac STS in his mother's driveway and hopped into his '63 drop-top Impala. He maneuvered through the intersection of Baseline and Mount Vernon like a man who owned the city. Mack was a hustler on the rise. He had street credentials that proved his stature in the eyes of all the players in the game. Though gangbanging wasn't his forte, Mack was respected by all the affiliates as a straight-up dude. Mack's theory was: *It doesn't matter what a person represents or what he's into, if he's trying to get paid, I'll mess with him.* This attitude helped him get far in life, especially coming out of the neighborhood that he grew up in. Now, and with much persistence, his cocaine dealings stretched from San Bernardino all the way to Oklahoma City.

Big Mack was, in a sense, a good person to know if you were a hustler trying to get paid. He was known for fronting a person a sack of drugs on consignment if they didn't have anything to get started. Today was a very special day for him because his little protégé was turning seventeen. Big Mack wanted to spend some quality time with him to let him know that he was proud that he had come so far. Just as he spun his steering wheel into the gutter lane, his cell phone rang.

"Hello?"

"Macarthur? Boy, where are you at?"

It was his mother.

"I'm on Baseline about to go pick up L'il Ray."

"Where did you leave my baby, Macarthur?" she asked in a concerned voice.

Mack stuttered, "He's around the corner from you,

Momma." Big Mack always knew to keep Ray near the 'hood so Ray could look after his mother. "Why, you haven't seen him today?"

"Boy, you know I've been at church all day. I just got in," she said, like he should have known better.

"Well," Mack hesitated, "when I pick him up I'll stop by the house and..."

"I won't be here. Sister McDowell and her daughter are coming to get me any minute."

Mack could tell by the rustling noise in the background that his mother was probably changing out of her church attire and into something more comfortable.

"I know," she continued, "that you guys probably have stuff to do today. Just tell my baby I'll see him tomorrow, and that I baked a German chocolate cake for him, all right?"

"All right, I'll tell him."

German chocolate cake, my foot! Big Mack thought as he got off the call. *I can't even get her to bake me a cake for my birthday!* He knew that ever since he'd brought Ray home in 1999, things had changed between his mother and him. The event that birthed his relationship with L'il Ray flashed in his mind as he rolled down Baseline. He remembered it like it was yesterday, and scenes shot like short clips of footage in his mind's eye.

*   *   *

Big Mack was hustling a well-known drug area in the streets of downtown San Bernardino. He was always known for keeping his appearance up to par, with his low cut temple fade and shadow trimmed beard. Anyone who took even a quick look at him knew he worked out diligently, because his six-foot, two hundred thirty-five-pound form was ripped and taut. Most people told him he resembled a cross between L.L. Cool J and Cuba Gooding,

Jr., and he dressed the part. Today was no different, and when he glanced down at his black Sean John outfit and buckskin Timberlands, he flicked a piece of lint off of his shirt.

Peaches, a well known prostitute, approached Big Mack at the Sara Motel just as he exited his room.

"Big Mack, babe," she began. "I need you to do me a favor."

Mack looked at her reluctantly. He could tell by the way she dressed and the stench that came from her body that she had been out there all night long. She still wore the same clothes from the day before — a red miniskirt and matching tube top, barely covering her breasts, which hung like old saddlebags. He closed his eyes at the sight of this thirty-year-old woman who wore a blond wig, and white high heel pumps that made her look every bit of five-foot-four. Her bright red lipstick reflected off her dark complexion like red Kool-Aid on a piece of white linen. Mack tentatively nodded.

"What kind of favor, Peaches?"

"Look," she continued. "Could you watch my son while I take this date?"

Mack hesitated. "Watch your..."

Peaches immediately interrupted. "Before you say no, I make six or seven hundred off of him. So you know he's caked up."

Mack looked at Peaches and thought, *I ain't no day care!* But he didn't show his feelings at that moment. "Peaches!" he barked. "Why you got that boy out here on the stroll, anyways?"

Impatiently, she replied, "My mom got sick again and my brother went back to Chino Prison on a violation. So, what else am I gonna do with him?"

Mack stared at the frustrated woman in disbelief. He couldn't believe the excuse she had just given him for having her son in that environment.

"Look, Big Mack," Peaches persisted. "I ain't come for a lecture. Thirty minutes max. Any longer and I'll send him out early."

Mack thought for a moment. "All right. But I want my cut."

"Your cut?"

"Yeah, and you'd better work your magic because if that trick goes over thirty minutes, send him out early...or I'll send your boy out to play in traffic."

Peaches stood with her legs spread apart, one hand on her hip. She smacked her teeth, making a hissing sound. "Dang, Mack! Why you wanna cut to do your girl a favor? You do me a favor right now," she said in a soft, seductive voice, "and maybe one night I can do you a special favor. You know that the game pays for itself, babe."

"Girl..." Mack shook his head, but was instantly interrupted by Peaches.

"All right, then let me hold a forty piece until I get back," she purred, but Peaches could tell by the look on Mack's face that she was pressing her luck.

"Get the money first, Peaches! All that tryin' to get high stuff can wait until you get finished."

"Big Mack, you be trippin' sometimes because you know I'mma spend the money with you anyways."

Mack just looked at her without any expression on his face. He shook his head. "Peaches..."

"Just hold on, Mack," she stuttered in frustration. Peaches called her son down from playing on the motel steps and instructed him to stay with Mack until she returned. "L'il Ray, babe, this is Big Mack, a close friend of mine."

"I know Big Mack, Momma," Ray said, reassuring her.

"All right then, babe, so you know you're in good hands, right?"

"Yes ma'am."

Mack looked at her son dressed in a dingy yellow shirt with orange stripes. The blue jeans that he wore had holes in the knees, and his shoes resembled what used to be a pair of Pro Keds. He shook his head. "What's up, L'il man?"

"Nothin' much," Ray responded, flashing a smile.

Still in disbelief, Mack stood and took notice of the small, frail boy again. His tattered clothing was filthy. His hair was uncombed and resembled the beginning stages of dreadlocks. His shoes looked as if they were four sizes too big. Mack thought twice about watching the boy. He knew that if he did, L'il Ray would have to get in his brand new Cutlass sitting on I-Roc rims, and he didn't want the filth off the boy's clothes to get on the car's interior.

As Peaches turned to walk up the stairs, she looked over her shoulder at Mack, who seemed unhappy about the whole thing.

"Mack, make sure you take care of my boy," she said, making sure Mack didn't change his mind. "I'll be back in thirty minutes, max."

Mack shook his head again and smiled at her. "He's cool. Come on L'il man," he said to the boy. "You wanna roll with me to get some burgers?"

"Yeah, Mickey Dee's!" he exclaimed, with a big smile and clenched fist.

"Speaking of Mickey Dee's, how did you know my name, anyways?"

Ray looked at Mack and said, "All night long while I'm playin' in the parkin' lot, people be sayin' your name. Big Mack this and Big Mack that. Everybody know you! I see you a lot, because a lot of people come lookin' for you."

Mack thought about how obvious the traffic was from doing business. He knew that the area was infested with a lot of dealers and addicts hanging out on every corner. He retrieved a beach towel from his trunk and placed it over his passenger's seat for the boy to sit on. As soon as he and Ray were settled in, he started the engine, cut up his stereo, bobbed his head as Tupac's "Dear Momma" came blaring through his speakers, and backed out of the parking lot.

When they pulled into the McDonald's drive-thru, Big Mack looked at the boy's malnourished frame and felt that he could really use a good meal. He shook his head as he looked down, seeing the innocence in Ray's eyes. His heart wouldn't remain firm, realizing that this kid was a victim of his circumstances. He smiled as Ray's eyes met his.

"When's the last time you've eaten, L'il man?" Mack asked curiously.

Ray responded by shrugging his shoulders.

Big Mack paused for a few seconds before he spoke. "What do you mean, you don't know? Did Peaches feed you last night?"

"No," Ray answered in a seven-year-old's low, soft voice. "I was sittin' on the steps waitin' on her to bring me somethin' to eat, and I fell asleep."

Mack's heart dropped. Queasiness entered his stomach. "You fell asleep on the steps without eatin', L'il man?"

Ray paused, then nodded. "I always go to sleep when I'm hungry because it makes it stop hurtin'."

Mack looked confused as a chill ran down his arm. "Makes what stop hurtin'?"

"This," Ray answered as he touched his stomach.

Mack was lost for words as he watched Ray's little dirty hand touch his stomach. He knew about the situation with his grandmother and uncle. But there had to be someone else who could take care of him, he thought. "Where's your dad at?"

Ray dropped his eyes and shrugged his shoulders again. In a little kid's voice he whispered, "My Momma said she's my momma and daddy."

Mack looked up as he pulled forward to stop again directly in front of the drive-thru speaker. He exhaled as he reached over and placed one hand on top of Ray's head as if to comfort him. "Don't worry L'il man, I got you. If ever you're out there again and you get hungry and sleepy, just come find me and I'll make sure you got somethin' to eat and a place to sleep, all right?"

Ray nodded and smiled.

"Now order whatever you want," Mack said, "before we get kicked out of this drive-thru."

After leaving McDonald's, they drove through a few neighborhoods that Mack occasionally hustled. He was hoping to gather up some of the loose money that people still owed him. Being so close to his neighborhood, he figured that it would be a good idea to stop by his mother's house to check on her. As he pulled in front of her yellow stuccoed house, which looked like it had been built in the seventies, Mack spotted her working in the flowerbed. She was on her hands and knees, which were covered in dirt.

"Hey, Ma!" he hollered out from the driver's side window.

His mother looked up and balanced herself against the railing of the porch. She stood up to stretch her back and said, "Now, I knew that was you coming when I heard that *boom, boom, boom!* rap racket."

Mack smiled at the sight of his mother patting her hands in midair as if she were beating drums. "What you doin' now?"

She always stayed busy doing something, and she knew that Mack was interested in whatever it was. "Oh, well I'm redoing my flowerbed." After she said this, her attention was immediately drawn to the little boy that sat in the passenger's seat. "Well, hello," she said, walking closer.

"Hello," Ray answered, mesmerized by the woman, who resembled Oprah Winfrey.

"What's your name?"

"L'il Ray," he answered in an innocent voice.

She looked at Mack, hesitated, then said, "Who's this, Mack? Is he one of your girlfriends' sons?"

Mack thought about Peaches and rolled his eyes. Ahhh…no, ma'am."

She could read between the lines. "Well, Little Ray, my name is Mrs. Wilson. I'm Macarthur's mom."

Ray smiled. "Nice to meet you, Momma Wilson."

Just hearing how he said her name made her smile. "Mack, he's a cute little boy. Ray, you're gonna have to come back and visit me sometime, okay?"

Ray's smile stretched even wider. "Okay."

"Mack," she continued, "I know you're just checking on me and probably won't stay long, but that's okay. Before I forget, that girl Tanisha stopped by here looking for you earlier. I was in the back and she was just knocking on the door so hard — beating on it, actually. I just wanted you to tell her to use the doorbell next time. I thought she was the police."

Mack laughed. "I got'chu, Moms," he assured her. "I'll be goin' away this weekend for a couple of days. Could you call Uncle Jimmy and ask him to pick up my car while I'm gone? I need him to change my brake pads for me."

Mack's uncle was a mechanic who owned a shop on Baseline. He liked to get high every now and then. And instead of him having to pay cash for Jimmy's services, Mack would just give him a gram of cocaine to pacify him.

Mrs. Wilson smiled as she wiped the sweat from her brow. "I'll tell him, baby."

Big Mack looked at his mother. "Is everything else all right?" he asked in a concerned tone.

"Yeah, I'm fine…" she assured him. "If you stop by tonight when I get back from choir rehearsal, I'll make some homemade biscuits smothered with chicken and gravy."

Mack smiled. That was his favorite meal. "That's a

date, Momma."

"And bring your little friend with you," she said, winking at Ray, who smiled and winked back.

I don't think so, Mack thought. He said his farewells and headed back to the motel with Ray, nothing but money on his mind. Pulling into the parking lot, Mack noticed the door of the room Peaches had walked into earlier was wide open. *Honk! Honk! Honk!* Mack blew his horn. He parked his car and told Ray to run up the stairs to let his mother know it was time to come see him.

As he gathered the wrappers and dusted off the crumbs that littered his car, his cell phone rang. "Wusss up?"

"Mack, I've been all over your momma's house lookin' for you!"

It was Tanisha.

"I know," Mack said, laughing. "She told me you were beatin' so hard on the door that she thought you were the police." As Mack spoke, he looked up toward the room again, and saw Ray standing in front of the door. It was still open. "L'il Ray, where's your momma?" he called out over the phone call.

"Who's momma you lookin' for, Mack?" Tanisha exclaimed curiously.

Big Mack got out of the car and walked up the motel steps, conversing with Tanisha along the way. "Look babe, I'mma come scoop you up tonight, okay? I'm out at the 'tel and I really can't talk right now."

Feeling as if Mack was doing something he should not have been doing, Tanisha said, "What do you mean you can't talk? Mack, did you say you were at the motel? With who?"

As Mack approached Ray, the boy turned his head toward him with tears in his eyes. "It's my momma, Big Mack. Look at her."

Mack directed his attention inside the room and

jumped instantly at what he saw. Peaches was lying naked in a pool of blood. Big Mack shook his head in disbelief at the sight of her body, which was covered with stab wounds to her face, neck, and chest.

"Man! I gotta call you back Tanisha..."

"But Mack —" she tried to say, but was instantly greeted by the dial tone.

Big Mack turned to Ray. "Go and get back in the car, now!"

Mack continued to take in the scene as his memory photographed every detail. Blood sprinkled the walls and soaked the carpet. The telephone receiver was busted, and since it was smeared, Mack figured it had been used to batter the woman.

"Dear God," Mack uttered under his breath as he dialed for an ambulance.

Chapter Three

Big Mack swerved around potholes as he drove down Baseline, his right hand gently caressing the steering wheel. The events that had occurred seven years earlier sometimes haunted him like a ghost from the past, and as he drove, he reflected on that dreary day. And just as he reached Medical Center Drive, he came back to his senses in time to make his intended right turn. Mack passed a patrol car that had pulled over a candy burnt-orange El Camino that sat on gold Daytons. The driver of the vehicle was a familiar associate of Mack's, a guy by the name of Bubble Up. Knowing Bubble Up well, Mack was certain that his partner was still riding around without a driver's license, gambling that he wouldn't get caught. He would undoubtedly have another car impounded, sittin' for another thirty days, Mack thought.

As Big Mack made a left turn on Magnolia, he entered his neighborhood and waved at the people standing on the corner and sitting on porches before he made a left turn on Flores Street. He pulled up to the curb, parked his '63 Impala, and jumped out just in time to catch a heated dice game. At center stage was Ray.

"Bet back or what?" Ray asked.

At five-ten and weighing one sixty, Ray stood there wearing at least ten inches of French braided hair that hung past his shoulders. He was posted up on the block. Big Mack walked up and laughed at him. His little protégé was a true hustler, just like himself.

The man who had just lost his money to Ray decided to give his luck another try. As soon as he dropped his money, Ray schooled, shook, and shot the dice like a professional crapologist. "Hit dice!" he called, snapping his fingers.

When the dice stopped their clattering somersaults,

the pair of ivories rested on trey four.

"Bet back?" Ray asked, as if it were the polite thing to do. He knew that a person who had just lost another fifty dollars usually tried to get his money back. "What's up homie...you in?"

"I'm cool," the man said with no intention of losing any more money.

"Shoot! I got you faded."

The man who had just accepted Ray's offer was his number-one road dog from the neighborhood. His skin was so dark that it looked jet black. His eyes were beady and red, as if he hadn't slept for a week, or had been smoking marijuana all day long. His lips were full and ashy, as if he were experiencing cotton mouth from the marijuana he'd smoked. And his nose — his nose seemed extra large for his face. Ray stared at his friend, nicknamed C-Dog, who stood over him with frizzy, two-inch braids. He nodded and smirked slightly at him. They had become friends around five years ago when Ray saved him from almost getting killed by a crazed junkie. C-Dog had just sold the addict a fake piece of dope when Ray happened to walk up on the incident. C-Dog was startled when the junkie pulled out a switchblade with a red engraved handle that resembled a fishing knife. But, as soon as the junkie took the knife from his pocket, Ray immediately withdrew his .25 caliber automatic from his pocket and aimed it directly at the side of the junkie's head. It was a gun he had found in the bushes one day after trying to hide from a truancy officer. He pointed it at the junkie and instructed him to leave C-Dog alone. The fiend did as he was instructed after seeing the look in Ray's eyes. Ever since that day, Ray and C-Dog had been tight as a knot.

Now, as C-Dog dropped two twenties and a ten to try to put an end to Ray's lucky streak, he watched as the dice skipped across the concrete, instantly converting his money into Ray's.

"No hard feelings, homie," Ray said with a smile. "This is all business.. .nothin' personal. Anymore vics?"

"Hey, lil' fool. Shoot fifty, bet fifty!" a challenge came from behind him.

Ray turned and saw that it was Little Donald. Little Donald was from the east side of town, an area called Little Africa. Ray saw him standing there, wearing black khakis with a black Raiders pullover, and accepted the offer by placing an additional fifty dollars on the ground. Then, performing his ritual school-shake-shoot, Ray watched as Little Donald reached to catch the dice before they stopped tumbling.

"Gimme these!" he exclaimed aggressively.

Ray readjusted his shot by picking up the dice with his thumb and middle finger. He palmed, shook, and threw the ivories in the air and watched as they came to a tumbling halt on ace-five.

"Bet the six-eight," Ray snapped, looking up at Little Donald, who instantly dropped an additional fifty dollars. Ray shook the dice once more.

"Gimme these," Little Donald said before they stopped.

Ray picked up the dice in perfect stride and shot them again. "Deuce-four, money gone!" he shouted at Little Donald.

"What the...? Man, I caught those dice," Little Donald insisted in a threatening tone.

With no expression on his face, Ray looked at the man. "Man, you caught the ones before that," he said as calm as he could. "Like I said, dawg, money gone," he exclaimed as he picked up his winnings.

Little Donald gritted his teeth, displaying a frown like a pit bull with rabies. "You got me messed up, if you..."

Before he could finish his sentence, Ray brandished a Colt .45 handgun that he kept concealed on the inside of his Averx jacket. He pointed the dime-sized barrel to the middle of Little Donald's chest and said, "First of all, I don't have you messed up. I got you figured out. Your best bet is to take that slow game back to the Eastside before I blow you back, fool!!"

Little Donald instantly got the message. He eased backwards, making tracks to his grey, primered, four-door Malibu. After he got in and started the car, he drove off, leaving skid marks in the street and a trail of smoke following.

As he put his pistol back inside his Averx, Ray noticed Mack. "Big Mack, what's up, homie?" he asked as he walked over to greet him.

"That dude L'il Donald is still try'nah slide through here with that drama, I see," Mack said, shaking his head. "Last time he came through here, Looney almost beat his brains in over shootin' loaded dice."

Ray unraveled, straightened, and counted his winnings while he talked. "Yeah, I know. I was out here that day. He hit Looney for a couple of G's." Then, as a afterthought, Ray asked, "Have you stopped by Momma Wilson's?"

"I just got off the phone with her. She just got back from church and was on her way back out with Sister McDowell. She said something about German chocolate cake."

The mention of the cake caused Ray to pause. He smiled at the thought, because it was his favorite cake, and Momma Wilson knew it.

Chapter Four

Ever since Ray's mother died, Big Mack and his mother had been taking care of the boy. Although Mack was always preoccupied with hustling, he convinced his mother to let Ray stay with her. After Big Mack explained what had happened at the motel, she conceded, and told him that Child Protective Services should be notified. Mack left everything up to his mother, stepped aside, and watched as she and a social worker made arrangements for Ray to be her responsibility. They did this because Peaches' mother was seriously ill and her brother was in jail. Within months, Mrs. Wilson had enrolled Ray in the 4th grade. That lasted every bit of three weeks.

In the three weeks Ray was enrolled in school, he was picked up by truancy officers thirteen times. He fought and cursed. And when the school bully tried to take away Ray's lunch money one day, Ray almost bit the bully's finger off while a teacher tried to break them up. It was Ray's second fight in two days, so Mrs. Wilson had to be notified and Ray had to be taken out of public school.

When she picked him up from school, all Ray could say for himself was, "I'm sorry, Momma Wilson."

Momma Wilson arranged home schooling for Ray, which went very well, except for math. Ray faithfully did his homework and, when finished, he was allowed to play in the neighborhood. But it didn't take long before he picked up on what the 'hood had to offer him. By the time he turned eleven years old, he had smoked his first joint. And by the middle of that year he'd seen his fourth dead body. By the age of twelve he had shot his first gun, a .25 caliber automatic that he found in the bushes. At the age of thirteen, he was arrested for the first time. He had a small bag of weed in his pocket. At the young age of fourteen, he was well-known throughout his neighborhood as a young hustler. All the dope fiends and junkies knew that he would always be in pocket.

One day after Ray turned fifteen, Momma Wilson called him into the house. "Ray, baby," she called out to the corner. "Come in here for a minute. I need to talk to you."

When Ray came into the house, he found her sitting in the den on her favorite love seat.

"Come sit next to me," she said with concern in her voice.

Ray did as she asked and looked her directly in the eyes. "What's wrong, Momma Wilson?"

She studied him before she spoke. "Ray, I just wanted to talk to you about a few things. You know, you've been with us for eight years now and I just wanted you to know that you are a part of our family and I love you very much."

"I know, Momma Wilson," Ray said humbly.

"Good, and I'm glad, because you've became sooo important to me," she said with emphasis. "Since your mother passed away, I've watched as you've gone through so many changes. But, what I want you to know is that we all go through these things in life called struggles. These struggles are meant to make us stronger. God uses them to help build us up."

"I hear you, Momma," Ray interjected. "But I'm not strugglin'," he said proudly.

"Baby, you're struggling whether you realize it or not. Just because you've found a way to keep a couple of dollars in your pocket doesn't mean that you're not struggling. I see how you carry yourself out there in those streets. I can't see everything, but I've seen enough to know that you're doing stuff out there that you shouldn't be doing. That worries me, son, because I know a man can't keep living his life on the edge and not slip or fall over."

"Momma, I'm cool. I ain't..."

Mrs. Wilson interjected by raising her hand in a

gesture for him to let her finish talking. She smirked. "Son, it's a cold world out there in those streets without God. And I want you to remember something, and listen well. I can't tell you who to hang with or who to befriend, but Momma Wilson has been around a long time. That boy Clayton that you run with...I know his family and they're a scandalous bunch of people. Just watch who you so easily call a friend, because everyone that smiles in your face ain't one."

Those words stuck with Ray, even though he didn't want to hear anything about a God who allowed his mother to be killed. And from that day forward he lived by three rules: Protect your family, get money, and watch everybody.

* * *

Ray thought about his money as he counted his winnings. Twenty-seven hundred dollars. Not bad. "Yeah, Mack, they donated a few G's to ya' boy for his birthday. What'chu got for me, big homie?"

Mack smiled at his protégé. He reached into his pocket and withdrew a sandwich bag full of Purple Kush and tossed it to Ray. "Roll somethin'," he said. "Terri and Trena are throwin' you a party tonight and asked me to bring you over. All the homies from the Westside is gonna come."

This interested Ray. "Cool, let's roll! But first, stop by Manuel's spot. He told me to slide through and he'll give me that tattoo I've been talkin' about."

Big Mack agreed and they hopped into his Impala. Manuel was a close friend of theirs, and he was well-known throughout the Inland Empire as a talented tattoo artist. Ray had never gotten a tattoo, but he trusted Manuel's skills. Now, as he and Mack drove down Medical Center toward 10th Street, they entered an area called the Projects. After Big Mack made his first right turn, they saw

Manuel sitting on his porch, relaxing.

"What's up, Mannie?" Mack hollered as he jumped out of his car.

"Nothin' much," Manuel replied. "What's up with you fools?"

Ray opened the passenger's door of the vehicle, slit the side of a cigar, and emptied out the tobacco onto the curb. "Yo Mannie, hook ya' boy up with that tattoo we talked about for his birthday."

"No *problema*," Manuel responded.

Mack approached Manuel and spoke in a whisper. "Can I get at you for a minute?"

Manuel saw that Big Mack meant business. "Sure."

Ray walked up to the porch while Mack spoke with his friend.

"I'm try'nah do what we talked about on those ten bricks as soon as possible. But...I need you to see if you can hook me up like we talked about."

Manuel nodded in agreement and asked him to hold on while he went inside to make a call. Five minutes later, he returned to find Ray and Mack sitting on the porch smoking.

"Is right now cool for you?" he asked Mack.

Mack exhaled a cloud of white smoke. "The sooner the better," he replied.

"Okay, look. You're gonna have to take a trip up to G Street and Baseline, by the music store. My cousin will meet you there. He'll be in an old white Datsun truck. His name is Rico."

Mack turned to Ray and said, "Look, I got to take care of some business. I'll be back to scoop you up in an hour or so."

"Cool," Ray said as he followed Manuel inside the house.

* * *

Big Mack made his way to the area where he was supposed to meet the connection. As soon as he entered the parking lot he noticed a white truck parked beside Groove Time Record Store. He parked next to the truck and nodded at the man sitting behind the wheel. The man stepped out of his vehicle and got into Mack's car

"What's up?" Mack said, looking at the man who stood about five-five and weighed in at about 210. Before saying anything else, Mack observed the connection closely, taking in the ponytail that hung past his shoulders, cleanly shaved face, the ostrich skin belt with the big buckle that held up his jeans, and the matching cowboy boots. "You Rico?"

"Look," the man said with a straight face and in a broken accent. "I don't know you. Manuel's my cousin, but I'm very *caucion*. Please don't be offended, but I do this for...how do you say? Umm...precaution." Rico pulled out a 9 mm Ruger and continued speaking to an unfazed Big Mack. "Now, my friend, ten kilos will cost you a hundred and thirty five G's. That's the price if you have all the money right now. That's at thirteen-five apiece, which is a good deal."

Real good deal, Mack thought. Taking his time to calculate his profits, Big Mack sat for a moment, then finally said, "I respect your precaution. Manuel told me that he could hook it up where I could give you half now and then an extra ten thousand on the other half when I'm finished."

"Manuel explained everything to me, and I's willing to do business. But to me...*trusa* is everything. I's need no one in my business. The product sells itself. I's be plain with you. I's give you one week to have the rest of the money. If you disappear and no show up, I's find you."

Mack sat in his car and leaned back in his seat, contemplating his next words. He needed this connection and he wanted the man to know that he was serious about doing business. "Listen," he began. "Not only do I have half now, but I'm willin' to give you my car here. This '63 Impala you can hold as collateral until I have the rest. Like you said, trust is everything, so just make sure she doesn't get a scratch on her. If she does...I'll find you."

Rico looked at Big Mack for a moment with a look of sincerity in his eyes, then began to laugh uncontrollably. Putting his gun out of sight, he nodded. "I like you. It's hard to do good business in a game with so many untrustin' people runnin' around. I feel we'll do good business, no? And no need for your car, *compadre*, or anymore threats. Follow me."

*   *   *

Manuel had just finished putting the finishing touches on Ray's tattoo when Big Mack knocked on the door.

"Everything cool? Did it work out all right?" Manuel asked, as if he hadn't heard from his cousin.

"Yeah, I'm straight," Mack responded. "What's up with you, birthday boy? You finished?"

Ray nodded, turning around to display his naked back to Big Mack. "What'chu think?"

Manuel had properly designed a tip-shaded outline of the words *Without Struggle There is No Progress*, with detailed artwork of the scales of justice in the midst of it. Mack looked closer and noticed that in the bowls that hung from the scale the word *Life* was in one bowl, and *Death* was in the other. *Your Choice* was written in the engraving on the scale's base.

"Yeah, L'il Ray, that's right! I like that. We all gotta choose how we're gonna live." Mack looked at his friend, who was still cleaning his tattoo gun. "So, what's up Mannie, what do I owe you?"

"Just shoot me some of that good green. The rest is on me for the homie's birthday."

"Bet," Mack agreed, instructing Ray to hook him up.

After the exchange a few more words of appreciation were said, Ray and Mack hopped back into Mack's car and headed toward the freeway. Mack made his way onto the I-10 on-ramp. "Ray, I'mma take you to Ontario Mills Mall to hook you up with some new clothes. It's your birthday, homie. Shop until you drop!"

"Look, Mack," Ray began as they drove down the I-10 freeway toward Ontario. "It's about time you let me in on some of those moves you be puttin' down out of state. I'm tired of playin' the corner. I want the nice house with the Lexus, Benz, and 4x4 truck like you had and ain't no other way people like us can get it but one way. I'm ready, dawg. What's up?"

"Oh, that's what you think this game is about? Havin' a nice car and house?"

"What else is it?"

Mack sat erect in his seat. He looked at Ray and shook his head. He sounded disappointed. "I'm out here try'nah get ahead in life. This game is about try'nah get your hands on enough paper to open up a business so that a person doesn't have to keep takin' penitentiary chances. This game ain't about cars and houses, Ray. It's about hopin' that you're blessed and lucky enough to get in and out with enough money to set yourself up for the future. This here, Ray, ain't about havin' nice cars!"

Ray dropped his head, and in a humbled voice said, "Well, teach me the game. I don't have idols like Michael Jordan or Vince Young. You're the only one I wanna be like."

Mack looked at him, feeling disappointed and disgusted with himself. "Man, Ray," he began in a lighter tone. "I'm not the kind of person you want to look up to," he said, shaking his head. "I don't know what to do, man." He paused. "I'll tell you what. I really don't want you to get out here in this game like me because I don't want anything to happen to you. This thang ain't promised to any of us."

Ray exhaled. "Come on, Mack, I know I'm takin' a chance. But what's the difference between me takin' a chance on the corner in the 'hood, and me takin' a chance try'nah make some real money, like you?"

Big Mack smiled at Ray's persistence. "Man, I don't even wanna be out here, Ray. I don't wanna be here!"

Ray didn't respond. He sat staring at Mack with a pleading look in his eyes.

Mack sighed. "Besides, Momma will kill me if somethin' happens to you." He shook his head. "Man, if everything goes right on this play I got goin'…well, I'll let you in because at least I can keep an eye on you. Until then, just be cool and chill out."

Mack raised the windows on his convertible, tapped the switches to bring the car closer to the ground, and switched lanes. His trunk was beating out of control.

Chapter Five

"Oooh girl, it's 7:30 and people is pullin' up all on the grass!"

Terri had a habit of complaining about everything since she and Trena had moved away from the west side of town. Both girls were rushing in their attempt to get everything prepared for the party they were putting together for Ray's seventeenth birthday. Out of the two, Trena was the most excited.

"You can move out of the 'hood, but as long as the 'hood knows where you at, they comin' girl!" Trena yelled out of the kitchen.

They had been living in this rented house for only three weeks. Trena and Terri were relatively young. Terri, the older girl, was nineteen. Trena was seventeen and only had a couple of months to go before she graduated from high school. Her dad had agreed to let his daughter move out of the house because she insisted on moving closer to Cal State University at San Bernardino, which she would attend in the fall.

Now, responding to the invitation Terri and Trena had sent out, people from all over the city began exiting cars, congregating on the lawn and giving daps to each other. Guys and girls out of the projects, Delmann Heights, Little Zion Manor, and Gilbert Street had all shown up for the gathering. As Trena looked out of the kitchen window, she saw all the people she knew from California Gardens, as well as her own Magnolia Street neighborhood.

A knock on the door was answered by Trena as she found C-Dog and some more of her homeboys standing with him on the porch.

"What's up, Trena? I know you didn't just invite the homies! Where's the home girls?" C-Dog asked enthusiastically.

Trena looked at C-Dog, who wore a pair of blue khakis and a Polo T-shirt. She shook her head at him. "You guys are so disrespectful," she barked, still tripping on how they all parked their cars on the grass like they were still in the 'hood. "Man, I hope the neighbors don't get too mad, because we're gonna party tonight." Trena gave C-Dog a hug and stepped aside as he entered the house.

In the backyard, the smell of barbecue lingered in the air as burgers, hot dogs, and chicken roasted on the pit. Eighteen to twenty women dressed in shades of red, blue, yellow, and pink sashayed around in shorts, sandals, and halter tops.

"Ain't nobody seen L'il Ray and Big Mack," Trena asked looking around.

"I saw them earlier at the mall," a male voice answered. "They should be here soon."

In less than two hours the party was in full swing. The DJ was spinning a tune from R. Kelly's Chocolate Factory album. When Mack and Ray showed up, they entered the backyard without being noticed, just in time to catch some of their "gangsta-fied" homeboys doing their rendition of "the step."

"Ah, man! Look at C-Dog," Ray said, laughing at the way his friend boogied in the midst of the people who were dancing. The way C-Dog wore his hat tilted to the side made him stand out in the crowd; especially since dudes from their neighborhood didn't display their bandannas hanging out of their back left pockets.

"Yeah homie, ya' boy can step," C-Dog said, waving his hands in the air. "What's up, dawg?" he asked as he approached Ray, greeting him with half a hug.

"Happy B-day, homie," Terri said as she made it out of the crowd of steppers. "Either of you want a drink? We got E&J, gin and juice, Tanqueray, Remy, Pink Panties, and you know a party ain't right without 40s."

Mack decided he'd have a Tanqueray, while Ray

asked for gin and juice.

"Hey, L'il Ray," a guy named Speedy, who was from L.A. Denver Lanes, yelled at him. "Smoke somethin' wit'chu boy?"

Ray pulled his sack out of his pocket and smiled. "Only the best, dawg, only the best," Ray said, holding his sack in the air.

The DJ switched the mood by playing "Atomic Dog" and all the partygoers waved and bobbed in unison, singing "Bow-wow-wow Yippy-yo Yippy-yea."

"Hey, L'il Ray," Trena called in a welcoming tone.

Ray looked at her and took in an eyeful. Immediately, a smile came across his face as she walked toward him, resembling Regina King in the movie *This Christmas*. Her Baby Phat blue jean shorts displayed a picture of a gold cat on the front pocket, and her white halter top showed off her bellybutton ring, while her matching three-inch thong sandals complimented her French pedicure.

They had known each other since he had first started living with Big Mack and Momma Wilson. One day while he was running the streets, Ray saw Trena getting off the school bus. From that day forward, he'd had a childhood crush on her, and she knew it. But Trena used to look at him and laugh. She would call him names like "hoodlum" and "thug" while she ran off giggling with her friends. Since then, she had matured into a fine young woman.

Ray took a double-take at how her hip-hugging jean shorts fit her curvaceous body, and smiled again. "What's up, girl?"

Trena just smiled as she approached him.

"The party is off the hook," Ray continued smoothly. "Especially now that I've seen you," he added.

"Thank you," she said, stopping directly in front of him. She put her hands on her hips, and smiled some more.

"By the way, Happy Birthday."

Ray nodded. "Thanks."

"You might as well give me a hug," Trena said, opening her arms to welcome him with a friendly embrace. "Dang, boy!" she said, pushing him backwards. "I said a hug and you're try'nah get all fresh with me."

Ray placed one hand over his mouth to cover his smile. He slid in closer to her once again and said as calm as he could, "Tonight is my night, and my only wish is to wake up in the morning next to you."

Trena gave off a soft laugh and shook her head. "Is that right?" she questioned. "Well, tonight just started and tomorrow morning is a long way away," she said, laughing, leaving him standing by himself as she turned and walked in the direction of her friends.

"Here ya'll go," Terri said as she handed Big Mack and Ray their drinks.

"Good lookin' out," Mack said, tipping his drink in her direction. "Hey, Ray, peep game. I see ol' girl over there," he said referring to a girl named Sheila. "I gotta talk to her about some business. I'll catch back up with you in a minute."

Mack walked over to Sheila. He knew that she was one of the most important pieces needed to complete his distribution puzzle. For years now their relationship as homies, lovers, and business partners had enabled them to do a lot of business out of state. Sheila had an uncle in Oklahoma City by the name of Man, and Big Mack supplied him with drugs. Ever since they'd made their second trip in 2007, everything from that point forward was all profit.

Sheila stared Mack up and down, from head to toe, with a mischievous smile on her face. "What's up babe?" she asked seductively.

"Nothin', just checkin' on my girl," Mack responded in a low tone as his eyes roamed the hourglass shape of

Sheila's body. Her light complexion, green eyes, and long, silky black hair that hung past her shoulders made her one of the most sought after girls in the neighborhood, even though everyone knew she had been in a lot of one-night stands.

To Mack, Sheila was always on top of her game. She stayed fresh, riding in a nice car, and was always independent. The only thing he wished she would work on was her quick temper. Sheila would get upset at times and go off worse than some of the guys he knew. But to him, she was still his girl.

"We need to talk," he whispered in her ear. As soon as they stepped out of hearing distance from the others, Mack began. "Look, babe, I need you to call Man and tell him I got ten bricks. Ask him what can he do with it, and how fast."

Sheila looked at him with wide-eyes. "Ten bricks? As in ten kilos? You want me to take all that with me on the Greyhound?"

Mack nodded without saying a word.

"Babe, we ain't never moved nothin' that big! Where am I supposed to put all that work?"

Mack hesitated. "Listen, I got that. All that stuff we were doin' was small. This can be the beginnin' of somethin' sweet. We can't keep takin' penitentiary chances movin' one brick here and there. If we're gonna take chances, let's make sure we make bail and lawyer money."

"But..."

"Babe, there ain't no buts. Either we're in it to win it, or we might as well fold our hands and quit altogether. See, I figured we'll tell your uncle to let them go for twenty-four to twenty-six G's apiece. And we do that, we'll make anywhere from $240-$260,000 from our first turn-over. This game ain't gonna last forever, you feel me?"

Sheila contemplated his words. "And what's my cut?"

Mack seemed surprised. "Your cut! Have I ever messed you over?"

"Hold up, now," Sheila said, raising one finger in the air and rolling her neck. "First of all, I'm the one who'll get all day if I get caught. So that stuff about gettin' a lawyer and bail money sounds good and all, but this is straight up business. So, what am I riskin' my life for?"

Mack listened before he spoke. He couldn't believe that Sheila would question him about getting her fair share, as she always did.

"Same as you've been gettin'. Fair exchange ain't no robbery."

As Sheila heard this, she propped one hand on her hip and turned her lip up. "Mack, we ain't ever moved anything over a key. Plus, with all that dope comes more headaches. I figure since I got to take it and stay until my uncles finishes, I should at least get $2,500 for each one."

"Twenty-five hundred dollars?" Mack shook his head. "Girl, you crazy! You try'nah get over, ain't you?"

"Tsk! Get over! How the…"

"Listen. I promised you from the beginnin' that I would give you a stack a brick and I've done that, haven't I?"

Sheila mumbled. "A thousand dollars ain't nothin'."

"What was that?"

"Mack, that's not the point I'm try'nah make!"

"That *is* the point! Since you think I'm makin' a lil' more money, all of a sudden you don't think it's fair now? What I've always promised you is what I'mma make sure you get. So what's up?"

She looked into his eyes and knew that he was all business. "You make $240,000 or better and you can't see me with a measly twenty-five? It's like that? Ain't no love for a real one, is it? I deserve at least that much, Big Mack. But since you can't see me with it, then it's your loss, because this real one will always get hers one way or another."

As Mack walked through the slider that led to the backyard, he thought about how her attitude had begun to change. He noticed that the party was winding down. The tables were cleared. The fire in the pit had gone out. The DJ went Dirty South and played a throwback. "Get Low" came blaring through the speakers. Terri, Trena, Sheila, and her cousin Tangy made their way into everyone's view. Tangy hopped on top of the table that once held food and started dancing.

"Take it off! Take it off!"

When the men and women stood around chanting, Tangy took her cue and began unraveling the shawl she wore around her waist.

"Man, I gotta see this," Ray said excitedly, breaking through the group of men who congregated around the table to see Tangy's performance.

Just as Tangy started her dance, she stopped. "Psych!" she yelled out. "Ya'll crazy if you think I'mma get naked for you," she said, laughing.

All the girls started laughing at the men. Tangy hopped down from the table and walked up to Ray. "Hey, birthday boy," she said, her voice purring.

"Nope, not this one," Trena said, walking over to Ray, grabbing him by the seam of his jeans.

"Hey girl, what's up?" he asked, startled by Trena's sudden appearance. "You've been drinkin'?"

"Ray, you know I don't drink! All a girl gotta do is act like she's gonna take off her clothes and you'll lose your mind, huh? Well, I have somethin' she doesn't."

"What's that?"

"Class! And I was gonna show you how much but..."

"But what?"

"But you're gonna have to stick around to find out later. What's up?"

Ray looked at Trena and said, "Look, you're drunk. I can see you wanna play games tonight, but I ain't in the mood."

Trena smiled. "Boy, I told you that I don't drink. So, for your information, I'm far from bein' drunk. I made up my mind about you long before tonight. So, are you gonna hang around, or what?"

Ray could see that she was serious by the look in her eyes. "Don't trip, it's all good," he began. "I couldn't think of another place that I would rather spend my birthday. Let me go holla' at my boy and tell him he'll be riding home solo tonight." Ray walked over to where Mack and C-Dog were.

"Hey, Trena wanna holla at'chu boy tonight. I'll get back with you later."

"Cool," Mack said with a grin on his face. "I'll be around to snatch you up around nine in the morning. I know you're gonna be doin' some beggin' all night because she ain't givin' up nothin'," he said with a chuckle. "Just be ready when I get here because I'm thinkin' about takin' you up on that conversation we had earlier about you-know-what."

"Bet. I'll be ready," Ray assured and gave daps to Speedy and C-Dog.

After Tangy's tease, the mood was set and many people began coupling up.

"Where ya'll goin'?" someone said to the others.

"To the Oasis Motel on Mount Vernon," someone replied. "We're gonna post up there for the night. Get 'bout four rooms and do the thang!"

Terri had just begun cleaning up when she saw Sheila. "What you got goin' on tonight, girl?"

"Nothin'. About to have C-Dog drop me off at home. That's what I get for ridin' with somebody else," Sheila answered.

"Oooh! Like that, huh?" Terri asked with a devilish

grin.

"Girl, naw! I said drop me off. You know I'm too much for him," Sheila said, tracing the outline of her body with her hands. "I'll see you later, girl."

Trena walked into the kitchen and told Terri that she was going to be in her room for the rest of the night.

"I see you finally got that boy," Terri said with a grin.

"It ain't nothin' like that, girl. We're just gonna kick it, that's all," she responded as both of them giggled like schoolgirls.

*　　*　　*

Ray was sitting at the kitchen table when Trena entered the room from the side door that led from the backyard. He smiled as she stopped directly in front of the old linoleum style kitchen counter, which sat adjacent to the light wood-stained cabinets, porcelain sink, and wall that looked to be painted an almond white. Ray looked up at her and smiled as she held dirty utensils with outstretched arms, as if she didn't want to get any grease and dirt on her Baby Phat attire. She smiled back at him as she took several steps, then placed the utensils in the sink. She glanced out of the window that sat directly above the sink and into the vacant backyard, only to see pieces of litter and light waves of smoke coming from the remainder of the smoldering charcoal.

Trena shook her head at the sight of what she witnessed and turned to Ray, only to notice him fumbling with the salt and pepper shakers that sat comfortably on the smoked glass dinette.

"Come with me, boy," Trena said seductively, grabbing Ray's hand and leading him out of the kitchen and down a narrow hallway. She steered him into her room. "You can get comfortable."

Ray looked around the room at the cherry wood dressers that matched the bedpost and headboard, which were engraved with scrolls and backed the queen sized bed. On each side of the bed sat a small, wine-colored lamp on a nightstand. Black and burgundy curtains covered the only window, and the ruffles at the bottom gave the room a alluring feel. Ray continued looking around, admiring Trena's taste. He noticed that the small bedroom had its own bathroom, as well. "Nice, real nice," he whispered softly.

"Chill out and get comfortable," Trena repeated. "I've got a stereo in my closet and the CDs are in the nightstand next to the bed. I'mma get in the shower, all right?"

Ray nodded his approval, slipped out of his shoes and jacket, and tried to figure out what he was going to do with his pistol. After he decided that he would lay it on the nightstand beside the bed, Ray searched for the stereo and CDs. Retrieving the stereo, he rumbled through the dresser and settled on some Jodeci: Diary of a Mad Band.

Fifteen minutes passed before Trena exited the bathroom. Ray looked up to find her standing in the doorway dressed in a long cotton pajama bottom and a Tweety Bird shirt that covered her navel.

"Your turn," she said, softly, pointing at him.

Ray jumped up from the bed and eased past her, smelling the fresh herbal essence coming from her skin. They were close to the same height. Trena's dark chocolate skin glistened. "Are you goin' to help me?" he asked with a smirk.

Trena laughed. "Boy, naw. I'll just be in your way."

"Oh, no you won't," Ray insisted.

"L'il Ray, stop playin' and get in there!"

Ray chuckled. "I'm not playin'."

Trena shook her head and let out a soft laugh. "That's what I'm afraid of," she said, pushing him inside of the bathroom.

Ray stood in the bathroom laughing. *Man,* he thought, *I can't believe Trena's gonna give me some! All that actin' like she didn't like me and stuff all these years. Yeah, boy, I'm the man!* As he said this to himself, he looked into the mirror and flexed his chest.

The bathroom sink and tub were lined with candles that were lit, giving off the scent of cinnamon. Ray blew out the ones around the tub because he didn't want to set himself on fire. The drugs and alcohol he had consumed earlier made him paranoid. After he had taken a much needed bath, Ray exited the bathroom some twenty-five minutes later.

"Dang, boy, you stayed in there longer than I did," Trena joked.

Ray stood there in his boxers and tank top. He looked at Trena as she lay comfortable underneath the covers, watching a small colored television that sat catty-corner on her dresser.

It's on! Ray thought.

Trena turned toward him and noticed his scant attire.

"Come on and get underneath these covers before your skinny butt catches some type of deadly pneumonia."

"Hey, whatever you say," Ray replied with a grimace.

As soon as he slid beneath the soft comforter she quickly addressed him. "Look Ray, I don't want you to be upset with me because you have plans on gettin' some, but..."

Hearing this, Ray halfway halted from getting comfortable. "But what...what's the problem?"

Trena sat erect in her bed and gave him her full attention. "Ray, I've liked you ever since the fourth grade. I've always had this dream that one day me and you would get together."

Ray adjusted his weight on his elbow. "Okay, we're together. What's wrong now?"

"What's wrong?" Trena stopped midsentence, contemplating her thoughts. "What's wrong is that you don't respect women. I saw how you looked at Tangy when she was on that table. Ray, you gotta respect me because I'm not like my home girls."

He shook his head at what he was hearing. "Oh no, here we go."

"I know it sounds corny, but I do want someone who will respect me," she said in rebuttal, noticing that Ray's eyes were aimed toward the ceiling as if he wasn't listening. This bothered her. "Ray," she began as she backhanded him on his frail chest, which made a popping, echoing sound.

He grabbed his chest. "Girl why you..."

"I'm serious, Ray. I really like you and I know you've been try'nah get at me too." She looked at him. "Boy, you know you have!"

"Yeah, I've been tryin', but you been playin' hard to get."

She smiled innocently. "I wasn't try'nah play hard to get. I just don't wanna be like a lot of my friends who mess with dudes that only want them for one thing," she said, dropping her eyes. "A lot of my friends have kids by dudes that's locked up or that don't even claim their own kids. It's crazy because females my age who get pregnant don't even finish high school or attend college, and over eighty percent of them are unmarried and end up on welfare. Look at them, Ray! Look at my friends, because I don't want to end up like them with the deck stacked against me."

Ray was hesitant. "What do you mean, Trena?" he asked, lifting her head so that he could look her in the eyes. "I always liked you for the right reasons. I mean, I don't want you to get pregnant, but it's my birthday and I can't help but to think about...you know...and..."

"But see, that's exactly what I mean! You're in this for the fun of it, but what happens if I get pregnant? I'm more than a bangin' body, Ray. And ain't nobody ever been with me! Plus, if I get pregnant right now I'll really be at a disadvantage in life in the eyes of society. You know that one in every three girls my age is said to get pregnant at least once by the time they turn twenty? That's why givin' myself to someone can't be just a game or a temporary fix for someone's pleasure."

Ray was shocked. He didn't know that Trena was still a virgin. Although he did respect her in his own way, the alcohol and weed that he had smoked earlier had him confused.

"I don't understand. So what did you ask me to stick around for?"

"Because," she pouted. "I wanted to spend this special night with you. I didn't want you runnin' around after no trash. It's time you graduate to some class," she said, softly kissing him on the lips.

Tangy ain't no trash, he thought, but he didn't know what to say. He was really confused now. Here she was, saying she wanted him to respect her, but she was just... *Ooh...she, ooh this*, he thought, confused.

Trena's lips pressed softly against his again and then she withdrew. "I just want you to lay with me and hold me. I want you to see me as a lady and not somethin' you can find in an alley scattered against a wall."

Something about the way she said what she said made Ray feel for the first time that if he didn't listen to her, he would be missing out on something good.

She continued. "I don't want this to start and end in the same night. We've waited this long, just wait with me a little longer."

Ray looked into her dark brown eyes and said, "All right, girl, you got that. But we can't be playin' and touchin' like this," he insisted, pushing away. "I don't have that much self-control."

Trena laughed at the way he scooted to the edge of the bed. "You're crazy. But you still haven't answered my question. Do I have you?"

Ray looked at her without answering, shaking his head. Trena hit him again in the chest.

"Ooooouch!" he called out, then he paused and said, "Yeah, girl."

"Yeah girl, what?" she asked in a pouting but stern tone.

Ray smiled. "Girl, we need to see if we can get you a fight with Laila Ali, the way you punch."

She hit him again.

"Ouch! You got me girl. You got me!"

Trena's smile glowed. Ray had never seen a girl so beautiful. She leaned forward to pull him closer, but the thought of getting hit again made Ray jump completely out of bed.

"Ray," she said, laughing. "I'm not gonna hit on you anymore, I promise. Come on back to bed."

"Girl...ain't nothin' wrong with this floor. I'll sleep right here," he said jokingly.

Ray eventually did as she asked him to. Trena hit the remote to her CD player as Jodeci came seeping through her speakers. *What a way to spend a birthday*, he thought. But in his heart he was glad to be there.

Chapter Six

The following morning Ray awoke in Trena's bed to what sounded like someone arguing just outside the bedroom door. It startled him. He immediately sat erect in bed when he heard the thud of someone getting struck, followed by a brief cry for help. Ray jumped out of bed. As he reached for his pistol, the door came crashing open.

"Yeah boy, you lookin' for this?"

It was a woman dressed in all black with a red bandanna tied around her head to conceal the black hair tucked underneath. It was a woman armed with his Colt .45.

"What you doin', Sheila? What's this all about?" Ray asked aggressively.

Sheila raised the gun and pointed it directly at him. "What does it look like? I'm doin' what I do when nobody wants to give me mine!"

Ray was confused. "Give you yours?"

"You heard me! Now get up and put your clothes on, punk!"

Ray didn't want to believe what he was seeing. "Man, stop playin' and give me my gun before I..."

Sheila interjected. Her hands were shaking. "Before you what?" she barked, thrusting the gun in his face. "Yeah, I thought so. Now get up before I put one in you."

Ray put on his jeans and shoes. He was led out of the room with Sheila at his rear. As soon as he entered the hallway, he saw Trena lying on the floor with blood-matted hair. She was balled up in a fetal position, holding her head, her Tweety Bird shirt and cotton pajamas soaked with blood.

"Man, what did you do that for?" he asked, attempting to walk toward her. She was barely moaning.

Sheila didn't smile. "Your broad got fly at the

mouth, so I busted her upside the head. Now, you try to do somethin' stupid if you want to!" Sheila threatened.

Ray hesitated for a moment before he was shoved from behind and marched into the living room where he saw his longtime friend C-dog, dressed in the same blue khaki pants and Polo T-shirt as the night before, sitting on the couch.

"What's up, dawg?" C-Dog said with a grin on his face.

"You tell me, C-Dog! And tell your girl to get that gun up off of me while you at it," Ray said impatiently.

"Naw, homie. See, I can't do that. What this is is you're gonna give me those ten keys or both of you are gonna die," C-Dog said, as serious as he could sound.

"Oh, so that's how it is, homie? This is how you do your homeboys?" Ray asked as he tried to spit on C-Dog.

C-Dog ducked the ball of spit that was hurled his way. "Boy, look it here, look it here!" he screamed, frustrated. "I'll smoke you right now if you keep on runnin' your mouth, 'cause we really don't need you. Your best bet is to sit down and shut up!" he said as straightforward as he could.

"We! You and this 'hood rat are ridin' together like that against homies you've messed with since way back?"

"Boy, ain't no friends when it comes to business," Sheila interjected. "This game ain't promised to none of us," she said as aggressively as she could. "Now, sit down and shut up!" she insisted, shoving him into the recliner chair.

Ray sat down and tried to gather his thoughts, while outside the rumble of bass coming from a car's stereo system shook the house on its foundation.

"It's Big Mack!" C-Dog exclaimed as he peeped through the curtains, noticing the Black Raven STS pulling up in the driveway.

"Get behind the door," Sheila instructed C-Dog.

"Yeah, I got him," C-Dog said as he stepped behind the door. "You know that boy is kinda big, anyways," he remarked softly as he waited for a few seconds until he heard footsteps approaching the door.

Knock, Knock, Knock.

"Come in!"

Mack turned the doorknob and entered the house, only to be knocked over the head by the butt of C-Dog's gun.

"What the...!" Mack screamed as he crashed to the floor.

"Yeah, sucka, who gets the last laugh now?" the voice asked.

Big Mack knew that the voice sounded familiar, but he couldn't figure out which direction it was coming from. Through his blurred eyesight, Mack made out who the person was.

"What's goin' on, Sheila?" Mack asked, straining to speak.

Sheila smiled mischievously. "This is what's goin' on! You're gonna take me to where those ten bricks are, or you're gonna die right here!" she exclaimed in a playing-no-games tone.

"Girl, I ain't givin' you nothin'," Mack barked with conviction.

"Oh yeah? Think I'm playin'? I'll start by puttin' a bullet in your lil' brother's head over here," she responded, pointing her weapon at Ray.

Mack tried to focus. Though his eyesight was bleary, he noticed Ray sitting in the recliner with Sheila standing over him, pointing a handgun at his head.

"Hold up!" Mack said instantly.

"Yeah, dawg, get it right then. Where's the dope?" someone said to his rear.

Mack turned around to see C-Dog standing over him, pointing a handgun at his face.

"Don't be surprised, homie. That's how the game goes. You win some, you lose some. Now, where's that work at?" C-Dog demanded.

Mack was defeated. The day that he had feared the most had finally caught up to him. The day when a thirsty, no good, backstabbing bloodsucker would try to rob him. Still, Mack surveyed his surroundings, realizing that they had the upper hand. *C-Dog is right,* he thought, still braced by one knee. *Dang! You win some you lose some. That's the way the game goes.* "I got them in the car."

"You better not be playin' any games. If this is some type of joke, I'll smoke you, so help me God, in broad daylight!"

"Listen, dawg, they're in the car. We can go get them together."

"Let's get 'em then," C-Dog said with aggression.

"Wait a minute," Sheila said, feeling like something was wrong. She looked at C-Dog hesitantly. "If you run off on me," she began, massaging the butt of her gun. "Boy, I'll come find you, so help me!"

No honor amongst thieves, Ray thought as he lay uncomfortably in the recliner with a gun still to his head.

"Girl, shut up, I got this," C-Dog replied. "Let's go, Mack. Get up!"

C-Dog waited for Big Mack to get up off the floor. He then opened the door and they stepped out into the fresh air.

Ray turned around and looked at Sheila. "So this is how it's goin' down, huh? Is this how you goin' out?"

Sheila smacked her lips. "Boy, shut up!"

Ray laughed. "I just wanna be the first to tell you that I know C-Dog and you'll never get a crumb of that dope. Not alive, anyways," he said, trying to provoke her.

Ray knew that he had gotten her attention. He wanted to tempt her to look out the window, but it didn't work.

"You just need to worry about if you're gonna make it, boy," she mumbled, looking toward the door. "It's a shame, too," she said, shaking her head. "I would've loved to spend some time with you," she added seductively.

Ray laughed again, this time out loud. "Big Mack says you're nothin' but leftover trash. That your body is looser than a 4-x T-shirt on a baby midget."

Sheila hit him on the back of his head with the butt of his own pistol just as C-Dog and Big Mack came through the door. Mack looked at Ray holding his head with blood running down the side of his face. He shook his head and gritted his teeth at the sight of his little brother's blood. C-Dog, on the other hand, had a duffle bag in his hand and right then Ray knew that they had gotten what they wanted.

"It's all in there," C-Dog told Sheila. "Ten bricks, right?"

Sheila nodded her head. "Good," she added, walking over to where C-Dog was standing. She wanted to get as close to the bag as she could.

Ray caught eye contact with Big Mack, who shook his head slightly. *I know, Big Homie. It's all part of the game,* Ray thought.

"Now, get over there by L'il Ray," Sheila ordered Big Mack with a shove.

Ray kept his eye on C-Dog. He would bet his last dollar on what was going to come next. As Sheila continued to stand by the duffle bag, pointing the pistol toward them, she was totally blind to what was taking place behind her. C-Dog crept up beside her, placed his pistol to the side of her head, and pulled the trigger. The sound was deafening and the effects were horrible. The impact pushed Sheila's head into the wall. Her body collapsed as blood, bone, and brain matter trailed its descent. Sheila's body lay crumbled on the floor with one side of her head blown completely off.

"Dumb rat!" C-Dog exclaimed as he watched her body collapse. He walked up to Big Mack and Ray, who was still lying in the recliner. "Yeah, homie. Don't look surprised, now. Every dog has his day."

At that moment Mack knew that he had no other choice but to make his move. While C-Dog was trying to be dramatic about robbing them, Mack lunged forward, pushing the barrel of C-Dog's gun aside.

"Get off me, buster," C-Dog said, right before the sound of thunder ripped through the room a second time. Just as Ray was about to make his move, he realized what had happened. He couldn't believe it. Big Mack lay on the carpet, clutching his chest, his eyes wide open. His lips were moving and his legs were twitching. Where he took the slug, blood was flowing out dark red.

That was all Ray could take. He slowly walked toward C-Dog, confronting him. "Man you — "

That was all that Ray could say before the first slug hit him in his stomach. The next two he didn't even feel. Ray was knocked to the floor before he could get any further words out of his mouth. The last thoughts that crossed his mind were of Trena lying on the floor, and of Momma Wilson.

Chapter Seven

Flash!

The light was bright, swooshing overhead as Ray was ushered along on what felt like a rolling bed. People were hovering over him, making a fuss with panicked looks on their faces. The pain hit him like lightning. Then, blackness.

Flash!

A man with a mask on his face looked down on him. It registered that the man was a doctor. He saw something long and sharp in the man's hands, which were covered in blood. The pain hit him again...then the blackness.

* * *

"Can't you see he's in no condition to answer any questions?" Momma Wilson said, grabbing at one of the men.

The voice came to Ray from afar, but was enough to shake him from his drowsiness. He turned his head and did his best to focus his eyes, trying to see what all the commotion was about.

"Ma'am, please, we're just trying to do our job!"

"Well, heaven forbid! It's not like he's gonna jump up out of that bed and run off into the night in the condition he's in."

"Ma'am, we've seen crazier things. Believe me."

It didn't take Ray long to realize that Momma Wilson was having it out with two police officers. One was a white male who weighed approximately one-eighty. He stood about five-eleven and wore a crew cut as if he had just gotten out of the military. The other officer, with the bald head, resembled Lieutenant Macky from the TV show

"The Shield."

Look at her, Ray thought. *Goin' hard.*

His eyes roamed and he noticed that he was in a hospital room. IVs were stuck in his arms and patches that were attached to an EKG machine were taped to his chest. He felt bandages around his shoulder, midsection, and lower back.

Man, I'm messed up, he thought.

His movement caught the attention of the officers, who immediately stopped their explanations with Mrs. Wilson and made their way over toward the bed.

"James Ray Turner," the officer with the crew cut spoke as he stood to Ray's left. "We'd like to ask you a few questions."

In a low, weak tone, Ray responded, "About what?"

The officer on his right, the one who resembled Lt. Macky, shot Ray an impatient look and said, "We're not here to play any games with you, Little Ray. That is what they call you, right?"

Ray didn't respond.

The officer looked over his shoulder at Momma Wilson and then back at Ray. "We already know about the drug buy and how it went bad."

Drug buy, Ray thought, *what drug buy?* Right then he knew that these two officers were just fishing for evidence. "It seems like ya'll have it all figured out." Ray cleared his throat. "What you need me for?"

"Who shot you, Turner?" the officer with the crew cut asked with concern in his voice. "Who did this to you?"

Ray looked at Momma Wilson, who had a look of extreme concern in her eyes. He acknowledged her with a slight smile. "I don't know. I didn't see 'em."

"So that's how you're going to play it, are you?" Lt. Macky's lookalike questioned in disgust. "You expect us to believe that you were shot in the house where two people were murdered and a young lady by the name of Trena

Lucas was severely injured, and you saw nothing?" The officer reached out and placed his hand on the bandage that was wrapped around Ray's shoulder.

"Ahhh!" Ray screamed in pain.

"You think we don't know about that little warrant with the probation department..."

Momma Wilson couldn't just stand by and watch the officers anymore without saying something. "What do you think you're doing?" she cried out as she quickly approached them.

"Officers," the doctor called out as he entered the room, noticing the commotion. "I'm going to have to ask you to come back at a later time. Besides, the next time you decide to barge in here looking for information, I'd appreciate it if you would get my permission first," he said with a stern look on his face.

Ray looked at the man standing between him and the officers. He didn't appear to be a day over thirty-five years old, wore a long white coat, and had a stethoscope draped around his neck. His California tan, blonde hair, and deep blue eyes made him look like a surfer instead of a doctor.

"All right, Doc," the officer with the crew cut said, smiling slightly. "We didn't mean any harm," he added sincerely.

The doctor nodded and returned a smile without saying a word.

"Your P.O. will be in to see you soon, real soon, juvie!" Lt. Macky's lookalike snapped as they turned and walked out the door.

The pain was excruciating. The doctor told them that due to the bullet wounds that Ray had suffered, he would be restricted to a wheelchair for the next six months. Ray dreaded the idea, but Momma Wilson told him to be thankful that God had blessed him to see another day. Ray knew that she was right, as always, so he tried to get a grip on himself.

"Are you okay, baby?" Momma Wilson inquired.

Ray shook his head. "This pain, Momma," he moaned. "It won't stop."

"I'll get him something for the pain, Mrs. Wilson. It's almost time for his next dose of medication anyway," the doctor said, leaving the room.

Momma Wilson looked at Ray with tears in her eyes. She leaned forward and lightly placed her hand on each one of his bandages. A tear dropped. "Ray, baby, you are healed in the name of Jesus," she spoke softly, resting her hand on his chest. "I plead the blood of Jesus over you. From the top of your head to the soles of your feet, you are healed, in the name of Jesus. You will recover completely. You hear me?" she emphasized, as she wiped a tear away.

"Momma Wilson, I..."

"Ray, listen." Her voice trembled. "I've spent the last ten years on my knees, praying for you day and night, hoping that something like this wouldn't happen. But what I was scared of happening has happened to you guys anyways, and I'm sorry." Momma Wilson paused and wiped the tears from her eyes before she continued. "But the devil won't get the victory out of this because, just like Job, I know the God that I serve, too."

Ray just lay there staring at her, speechless.

Momma Wilson shook her head. "Baby..." She paused slightly. "You can't keep living like this. You have to change, you hear me?"

"Yes, ma'am," Ray agreed, not wanting Momma Wilson to worry anymore. But in the back of his mind he knew that he couldn't let everything that happened go that easy. He saw that everything was happening so fast, and he began to reminisce. C-Dog, Sheila, Trena, and.... "Momma Wilson," he began as if the thought had eluded him. But apparently the expression on his face gave him away because she answered before he could finish.

"He's dead, baby. Big Mack is...dead."

* * *

Sitting in Ray's hospital room with a blacked eye and a piece of white gauze taped to the side of her face, Trena attempted to cover up the thirteen stitches she received from being assaulted. Her hair was nicely feathered, and slightly styled to cover her eye. Ray looked at her as they conversed, taking in every detail of her essence. The way she wore her skinny jeans and cotton T-shirt that barely covered her belly ring, her French manicure and lack of makeup allowed him to see how strong and proud she really was. He smiled to himself at the thought of her being so courageous. But he still needed answers. He was still curious about what had transpired that fateful morning.

"And then what?"

Trena was sitting with Ray, going over everything that had transpired that morning when he and Big Mack had gotten shot. "You know, Ray, ever since that happened my father made me move back home and has been very protective of me. But..."

"Trena, but what?"

"But I don't know if he's gonna approve of us now that all of this has happened, you know?"

Ray had a confused look on his face. "Well, how about if I talk to him? I don't have anything left in my life to look forward to. You think if I..."

Trena interjected, "If you what? Ray, my dad is scared for my life right now. Plus, they haven't caught..."

"Hey!" Ray interrupted, looking over her shoulder as if looking for someone. "Trena, your dad doesn't have to be scared of nothin'. When I get out of here I'mma take care of him, believe that!"

Trena slumped her shoulders, letting out a heavy exhale. "Ray, that's exactly why he's afraid that somethin's gonna happen to me. The streets talk and that's what's bein' said out there."

"What's bein' said?"

Trena looked reluctant. "People say that C-Dog might as well be a dead man leavin' a witness. Especially you!"

Ray nodded. "Those people out there on the streets don't know me! Nobody knows who I truly am. And maybe he shouldn't have left me alive." Ray closed his eyes.

Trena just stared at him, quietly thinking about what her father had told her. "Ray, I thought I knew who you are. What about Momma Wilson? Does she know who you really are? Do you even know who you really are?"

Ray lay with his eyes closed, bobbing his head as if in deep thought.

Trena shrugged. "Maybe you don't know."

Ray still didn't respond.

"Does Mrs. Wilson know who did this to us?"

Ray opened his eyes. "I don't want her to know that C-Dog did this," he began to explain. "She'd go and tell the police and I'm not out there to protect her. You feel me?"

"Yeah, I hear you."

Ray could tell by the tone in her voice that Trena was worried. "You know, I was really thinkin' a lot about you these past few days," he said, trying to smile. "So, how you been?" he asked with a little more concern in his voice.

"Nervous," she admitted. "My dad won't even let me go anywhere by myself. I had to ask Mrs. Wilson to help me come up here. She didn't like the idea that I was gonna lie to do it, but if my dad knew I was comin' to see you..."

Ray tried to be understanding by nodding his head. He knew that her dad had come from the same streets, but he had made it out of the neighborhood before he got caught up like most people had.

"I'm just glad you're all right, Ray."

"Me too," he agreed with a slight smile on his face.

Trena sat with him for about an hour before Mrs. Wilson returned, this time with plastic plates wrapped in aluminum foil. Ray could smell the chicken as she walked in the room.

"Momma Wilson, what'chu got in there?" he asked, referring to the plates she was carrying.

Momma Wilson smiled. "Baby, I figured that I'd make you some real food today. I got you some smothered chicken, collard greens, macaroni and cheese, and you know Momma got you some homemade cornbread. You look so skinny."

Ray smiled as he responded, "I lost weight from the lead diet, not the hospital food," he said, trying to be humorous.

Mrs. Wilson looked baffled at what Ray had just said. Trena lightly shoved him on the arm, knowing what he was referring to.

"Ooooooouch!" Ray exaggerated.

"That's not funny, boy," Trena exclaimed.

The exchange of words confused Mrs. Wilson as she looked at both of them, and continued setting out the food on the hospital tray table.

Lead diet, Ray pondered. *I ate those bullets and I'll be back again! But this time I'll be serving the meal,* he thought. Ray shook his head as his jaws tightened. He lay there quietly as Trena helped Momma Wilson finish making their plates and setting the food on his tray table. The more he thought about what he had just said, his smirk began to fade. *Big Mack,* he thought. He couldn't help but to see Big Mack's face every time he looked at Momma Wilson. He closed his eyes, reminiscing, because he knew that this meal…this was one of Big Mack's favorites. Ray slowly opened his tear-filled eyes just as Momma Wilson and Trena finished setting up the food.

Momma Wilson rubbed her hands together and held them close to her lips. "Okay, baby," she began. "Let's thank the Lord before we eat."

Ray cleared his throat as his eyes continued to tear up. His heart was heavy and he spoke just above a whisper. "Momma, I'm sorry."

Momma Wilson's eyebrows touched each other as a curious look came over her face. She gently placed her hand on his chest and asked softly, "Sorry for what, Ray?"

A tear dropped from the corner of his eye as Trena stood listening out of curiosity. Ray's voice trembled as another tear rolled down his cheek. "Momma," he started, then hesitated. "For what happened to Big Mack. It was all my fault because he was comin' to pick me up and…"

"No, baby, no," Momma Wilson interjected, trying to hold back the tears that began to well in her eyes. She reached up toward his face and rubbed the tip of her finger across his cheek to wipe away the tears. She looked at Trena, whose eyes were now filled, and slowly pulled her close to them. "It wasn't your fault, Ray. It wasn't neither one of you guys' fault. God…"

Ray tried to interject. "But if…"

Momma Wilson instantly cut him off. She placed her hand over his mouth to silence him. She shook her head as her lips tightened. "Ray, God must have been ready for Big Mack. He couldn't have…have died if God didn't allow it. So, baby, it's not your fault. It's not your fault at all."

*   *   *

Knock…knock…knock, was the sound that echoed off the door.

"James Ray Turner! Remember me?"

Instantly the voice registered, but Ray couldn't believe what he was hearing. He continued to lay there on his hospital bed without movement, as if he were sound asleep.

"Oh, yeah, you remember!"

Ray knew that this day was coming. He opened his eyes to pay the piper. It was his crazy probation officer, Tom Upshaw. Upshaw was a middle-aged white man who reminded him of Adam Sandler and talked a lot of trash to everyone. Ray had been playing cat and mouse with him for the last six months, not reporting and dodging his telephone calls. Now, Upshaw had him red-handed.

"What's up homeboy?" Upshaw asked, as hip as he could, mimicking how most of the young black guys talked in the 'hood. "I see you all banged up in this thang. What did you take? Three, four or five, like ya' boy Tupac?"

Ray shook his head. "Three," he answered, a little disgusted with Upshaw's sense of humor.

Upshaw laughed. "Well, I figured since everybody else has you in their crosshairs, I'd roll up and take my best shot, too."

Ray knew it was coming, and all he did was think about how bad Upshaw's timing was.

"The Po-Po told me you went gangsta up in this thang. Said you didn't know jack. They called ya' boy, and here I goes."

Ray was irritated at this point by Upshaw's mimicking. "So what's up? Like I said, I don't know who shot me."

Officer Upshaw's demeanor became more serious. He stood there staring at Ray as he lay there in the hospital bed, looking pathetic, and said, "You know, Turner, I've been working cases for fifteen years and I know how it goes. The 'G-Code,' right? You don't wanna snitch. But what you and your young punks don't realize is that you've got a crazed nut running around with a gun who knows you're not dead. He expects you to come back and try to kill him, because he knows you won't tell."

Ray shook his head. *Another cop who's got it all figured out,* he thought.

"This fool," Upshaw continued, "soon will panic. He obviously knows who you are, and if he knows who you are, he knows where you're from. If he knows where you're from, he can find out where you live. And if he can find out where you live, there's a good possibility that more people besides yourself could be at risk."

Ray tried to act nonchalant, but his mind couldn't help but to shift to two people: Momma Wilson and Trena.

Upshaw stared at Ray, then shrugged his shoulders. "When I heard you got shot, I'm not going to lie, I thought I'd lost another young man to those streets out there. I didn't want to find you like that. Now, while it may seem like I've got you at a disadvantage, this time it's for a higher cause. When I lock you up, it's gonna be for your sake as well as those who love you."

Ray looked confused. "My sake? The people who love me?"

Upshaw nodded. "Yeah, for all your sakes. Before you get everybody killed."

That hurt. Ray couldn't believe that this man, someone who didn't even know him, someone who judged people by files that stayed in cabinets…that this man would even insinuate that he would be the reason for Momma Wilson or Trena to lose their lives.

"So, what'chu sayin', dawg?" Ray spat.

"What I'm sayin', homeboy, is that I think the year you've got left on probation would be best spent up in Norwalk."

"Norwalk!" Ray exclaimed. He knew Norwalk was a city in Los Angeles County, but he didn't understand its relevance.

Upshaw smiled at Ray. He knew Ray was headed to a correctional facility that housed juvenile offenders who were sentenced to do time. "Yeah, Norwalk! They got a little resort called Fred C. Nelles. That way I'll know for certain you'll have a chance to get'chu mind right before those streets get it right for you."

Officer Upshaw said this, turned on his heels, and headed toward the door. Ray's eyes followed Upshaw until he saw a uniformed police officer standing in the hallway. The officer turned and looked at Ray after talking to Upshaw.

They're gonna put a babysitter on me, Ray thought. Although he had known that this day was coming, he hadn't expected it so soon.

Chapter Eight

It had been a month since Ray had been shot, and ever since he got confirmation that he had violated his probation, he tried to savor every bit of his freedom. Momma Wilson was at the hospital every chance she got, and every other day she would bring Trena with her. However, every time they came to see him, Momma Wilson would leave for a few minutes to allow them to talk.

"So, what's the word out there on the streets?"

Trena looked over her shoulder as if to be looking for someone. "The latest is that C-Dog is drivin' a brand new Yukon Denali with limo tinted windows. They say he's been movin' in and out of state, pushin' a lot of dope. His mother said she doesn't want anything to do with him for some reason. They said somethin' about she didn't want to bring bad karma to her house or somethin' like that," Trena answered in a whisper.

Ray stared at her coldly. "Bad karma, huh?"

Trena nodded. "Ray, you can't keep…"

"Hey, Momma Wilson," Ray interrupted, changing the subject as Momma Wilson walked through the door. "Momma, how was…Big Mack's funeral?" he asked hesitantly.

"Baby," she began, clearing her throat. "Everybody came. It was very, very nice. A lot of your friends from the neighborhood asked about you and said that if they could they would come up here to see you. Fresh said he's been real busy with his music label and restaurant, but he said whatever you need him to do, just let him know. And, you know that boy, Bam, is wanted by the police? After I told him that they keep an officer outside of your door around the clock, he just said he sends his best."

"Is that right?" Ray said, undecidedly thinking

about Bam. *Some homeboy*, he thought.

*   *   *

When the day came for him to be released from the hospital, both Momma Wilson and Trena were present.

"Baby, don't worry about anything," Momma Wilson encouraged him. "That place you're going to is just a pen for little men," she said with a soft laugh. "We'll be able to see you real soon, okay?"

"Yeah," Trena assured him. "I don't know what I'mma tell my dad, but I'll get him to let me go."

"What do you mean you don't know what you're gonna tell him?" Momma Wilson questioned curiously. "Trena, I covered one time for you, but I can't do that anymore. What you're gonna tell him is the truth, you hear me?"

Trena dropped her head and Ray found that he was grateful that she said she would be by his side. *Class*, he thought.

"Just make sure you don't forget me," Ray expressed, looking at Trena.

"Boy, you'll only be gone for six months at the most. I could wait six years if I had to," she said with a confident smile. "You just don't drop the soap!"

Ray laughed because he knew what she was referring to. Trena looked at him and instantly raised her hand as if she were going to backhand him. Ray flinched. Even though he had been shot in his stomach, lower back, and another bullet had grazed his shoulder, he was glad the doctor said the bullets hadn't hit any main organs and that he should fully recover in six months. But still, getting punched by Trena was not something he wanted to experience at that moment.

"Boy," Trena said with a smirk. "I ain't gonna hit you anymore. I don't want you to think it's cool to start hittin' on me someday," she said, looking at Momma Wilson.

Momma Wilson smiled as all three of them laughed at how Ray had receded in his wheelchair when he thought he was about to get slugged. "Girl, I think you're a natural with this boy. Maybe you're exactly what he needs to keep him in line."

Both Momma Wilson and Trena shared another laugh while Ray twisted his lip in protest.

The next day Ray was released into the custody of his probation officer. A hearing had already been held in his absence to revoke his probation and he was being wheeled out of the hospital in a wheelchair. He was placed in an all white van, equipped with a lift on the side to help the disabled. Directly inside the van sat Officer Upshaw.

He chuckled. "Wait until you meet Fred. You'll love him!"

Ray knew that this was Upshaw's display of humor, so he allowed the comment to run off of him like water off a duck's back. He didn't see anything worth looking forward to. No streets, no money, no homeboys, and especially the number one thing: no get back! Ray just slumped in his wheelchair and enjoyed the ride.

The Southern California weather was perfect for an afternoon drive. "It Never Rains in Southern California" was playing on the radio. Ray didn't know why people thought that. Southern California saw more than its share of rain. But probably, he thought, it was days like this that made them write the song.

Although it wasn't raining literally, the closer they got to Norwalk, the more it felt like a storm was brewing. When the van pulled up to the property, Ray looked out the window at a group of young men. Some were working out, some were being led into a building in a single-file line, and others seemed to be doing chores. All eyes seemed to focus on the white van as it pulled onto the lot.

"Weeee're heeeeere!" Upshaw exclaimed.

Ray looked at Upshaw and shook his head. The correctional officer driving the van parked, and after getting some paperwork from Upshaw, he notified them that he would be back momentarily. This was when Upshaw turned to Ray.

"Yo' Turner!"

Ray really didn't feel like being humored. To him, this was a nightmare. "What's up, man?"

"I know this is not what you want right now, but you've got to listen to me." Upshaw gave Ray his most serious look and said, "A lot of kids are sent through this system and many just keep right on going until they find themselves locked up in Corcoran or Pelican Bay, or somewhere with a life sentence. Take my advice. Let this be a lesson for you. You'll be here for a few months, but if you use the time wisely, those few months could change your life."

Ray had heard all of this before. He was beginning to wonder why a person like Upshaw even cared.

"Me personally," he continued, "I'd rather see you behind a desk than behind a gun, but it's your choice. See, it'll be your decision to make whether you step out of here a man who will make Mrs. Wilson proud, or a man who will cause her more grief. I knew Macarthur. I was his probation officer eight years ago. No, he never went to the pen. He skated by. But in the end, the laws of the street caught up with him. Don't make those same mistakes, Turner. You can go in there and change, make something out of your life. You can do it for Mrs. Wilson — or you can do it for yourself. But you have a chance to get it right because you're still alive. Some people don't get this opportunity."

Officer Upshaw's words seemed to penetrate Ray's conscience. He stared at the man in disbelief because the words truly seemed to come from the man's heart. He knew Upshaw wasn't trying to be cool by mimicking the way he talked. He was serious.

Ray looked at him and said, "I hear you, man."

Upshaw smiled. "I don't want you to hear me, Turner. I want you to feel me."

Chapter Nine

Chills ran down Ray's spine as he and Upshaw entered the four-story stone building. There was a grey metal door adjacent to the right side of the building. The booming sound of heavy metal closing behind them caused him to wince as a metallic click-clack sound followed. *A sign of the doors being locked,* Ray thought.

Nervously, Ray's eyes roamed the 3,000-square-foot structure, which resembled a warehouse on the inside. He took in every detail, noticing the small, twin-sized beds lined up in rows. He glanced down and stared at the polished concrete floors, then dropped his head. He closed his eyes in disbelief over what he'd gotten himself into. He inhaled, then exhaled as the minty, chemical smell of Simple Green and fresh wax lingered in his nostrils. He partially opened his eyes. He could tell by the smell, and his mirrored image that reflected off of the floor, that someone had just finished cleaning and waxing it. He opened his eyes completely, then lifted his head until his eyes met a sign hanging on the wall directly in front of him: D-Unit.

D-Unit dormitory at Nelles housed approximately a hundred and twenty young men. And even though Upshaw had walked Ray through the initial stages of his orientation, he felt butterflies in his stomach when Upshaw left him in the hands of an older black officer. Ray glanced at the man, who stood about six-three, weighed about two-twenty, and seemed to be about fifty years old.

The officer looked down at Ray with no expression on his face. He shook his head. "Job security for sure," he said in a stern tone. "Kids like yourself is gonna always make sure I keep a job."

Ray was stunned. He had nothing to say in rebuttal.

"By the way, I'm Mr. Carney," the officer said as he

made Ray wheel himself across the building to the officers' station that sat in the room's center.

Ray looked up at him in awe. *He ain't got no heart,* Ray thought.

At the station, Ray was greeted by two more white correctional officers and a medium height, stocky black man who was around forty-five years old.

"What's up?" the black man said. "I'm Counselor Steele."

The man outstretched his hand for Ray to shake, but Ray didn't respond. He couldn't see himself shaking hands with the people who were holding him captive.

Counselor Steele smiled. "Okay, then. I see how this is gonna be. I'll be your counselor," the man continued, like Ray's rebuff was no big deal. He pulled back his outstretched hand. "You'll be assigned a bunk and we expect you to get along with the rest of the young men. No smokin', drinkin', cursin' and no fightin'. Is that clear?"

Ray nodded in agreement.

"The majority of the men here are in school, so we'll be lookin' to see if you finished high school or not."

School! Ray thought.

"What 'hood you claim?"

Ray tried to keep calm, cool, and collected as he side-stepped the question. "What days are visitin'?"

Steele giggled. "Friday, Saturday, and Sunday."

"All right," Ray told the man, hoping that he would put an end to his "Welcome to Fred C. Nelles" speech.

"I'll be gettin' with you soon for your first one-on-one. I expect to get to know you more then. In the meantime, I know it's not home, but try to make the most of this experience."

Counselor Steele walked away and one of the officers standing in front of Ray stepped forward and spoke aggressively. "Check it! Everybody will be back in about ten minutes. Counselor Steele told you the rules and we expect you to abide by them. I don't know where you're from or what 'hood you're claiming, but you can leave all that junk for the streets. In here there's no Crips, Bloods, Dirty White Boys, or Serranos. There are only men!"

Ray listened and took note on how everyone who worked there seemed adamant about stressing the point of gangs and neighborhoods. That let him know that gangs must be a big problem. What did they expect? This was California!

The housing unit officer showed him to the bunk that he was to sleep on, and Ray almost lost his cool. He couldn't believe he was expected to spend the next six months sleeping on a spring loaded bunk with a flimsy, four-inch mattress. He kept his thoughts to himself as the officer brought him a bedroll with towels, soap, deodorant, a mini toothbrush, and a tube of Mega Mint toothpaste.

"Make yourself at home," the officer told him.

That was something he'd never do. He didn't want to be there, but he had no other choice but to stick it out until the end. But makin' this place home? *Never!* he thought.

The officer walked away and left him to get himself together. He was still sore and moving was difficult at times. He was attempting to make his bed when he heard the sound of a lot of people coming into the building. He looked up and noticed that it was a group of guys who looked to be between the ages of twelve and nineteen, even though some of them could have been older.

There were Mexicans, Whites, Blacks, Native Americans, and Asians who all looked tired and worn out. They filed in through the doors, talking and making a lot of noise.

"Count time in thirty minutes," one of the officers yelled.

Ray looked up from his bunk where he found himself struggling with two sheets and a harsh, greenish-grey wool blanket.

It was a muscular, bald-headed officer who had yelled from his station in the middle of the dorm. The officer rubbed his palm across his bald head and continued. "If you're gonna hit the water, I suggest you do it now!"

The young men began moving like it was their normal routine. Many stopped by their beds for a split second and gave Ray a good looking over. Their faces said, "Who is this?" Ray just sat in his wheelchair and looked back at them. Just as he was taking in the scene, he felt someone approaching from behind.

"Man," the voice exclaimed. "I thought that was you, L'il Ray, what's up, homie?"

As he turned to look over his shoulder, Ray noticed who it was and found he was less than excited. Ray gave him a nod. "What's up, Poochie?"

"Man, this is crazy! Look at'chu, dawg."

Ray knew that he was referring to the wheelchair. Trena told him that the streets had been talking about how he had survived and Floater, who everyone called Poochie, was from his neighborhood. The chances were good that Floater knew everything about it.

"Yeah, man," Ray replied. "It ain't nothin' though. I'll make it."

Out of nowhere four more guys walked over to where they were talking.

"Yo'," Poochie said, nodding toward the gentlemen. "Do you remember the homie Joe-Joe?"

Ray looked up at the guy to see who Poochie was talking about. Joe-Joe was a short fat dude who was standing there wearing a T-shirt drenched in sweat. Immediately, Ray recognized exactly who he was. Joseph Calhoun.

"Yeah, Joe-Joe. Ain't you..."

Joe-Joe smiled. "Terri's cousin," he finished Ray's sentence. "I heard what happened, man."

Ray nodded. "Yeah, we'll chop it up."

"And this," Poochie continued, "is Tee. He's from the west side. 1-Punch, he's from the projects. And this is the homie Buff, from Riverside."

Ray made a gesturing nod.

"What's up," they all greeted in unison. "Yo', L'il Ray, I see you, soldier," the one called 1-Punch said.

Ray knew him. Even though Ray had never seen him get into a fight before, the rumor was 1-Punch had a reputation on the streets for being a bully. He had a wide stature with big knuckles. They made eye contact. Ray noticed as 1-Punch smiled at him and nodded. Ray recognized it as an acknowledgement for what he had been through.

"Yo," Buff began. "I'mma catch the shower before count. Nice to meet you, homie."

"You, too." Ray looked at the rest of the guys and then back to Buff. Right at that moment he noticed why they called him Buff. He must have been six three, two-twenty. He was indeed a big boy.

"Yo'! We need to get in there, too," 1-Punch, Tee, and Joe-Joe agreed.

They made their way to the showers. Poochie stayed with Ray to help him fix his bedding. He gave Ray the rundown about everything that went on around there.

"Breakfast is at six, lunch at eleven, and dinner's around five. All the homies try to stick together because there was a lot of set trippin' goin' on around here. There's a small beef goin' on between the Crips and the Bloods, but mostly it's between the Blacks and Mexicans. Ain't nothin' really happened yet," Poochie explained, "but you can feel it comin', homie."

Ray listened as Poochie continued to tell him how they had to be up by five-thirty every morning because they couldn't afford to be caught sleeping or still lying in bed if something happened between one of the rival gangs. He then told him about everything from visiting to the television shows they watched. He told him how one of their homeboys, Big Bird, had gotten into a scuffle two weeks ago and stabbed a boy out of Bakersfield in the neck with a pencil.

"They sent him back to County with more charges," Poochie added with a distant pause. "The word is that they're gonna charge him as an adult and send him to state prison."

As Poochie continued to tell Ray the stories of incarceration, he finished making up Ray's bed. Then, it was count time. He then helped Ray to his bed. Ray was eager to get out of his wheelchair and lie down. He was tired.

* * *

Ray didn't know how long he had been asleep, but it must've been a while. He had a nightmare about Big Mack getting shot and when he awoke covered in sweat, he realized it was much more than just a dream. Ray got up and instantly felt the pain from his healing wounds.

"Man, homie, you missed dinner." It was Poochie. "I didn't want to wake you, but don't trip. I got some commissary if you're hungry."

Ray rolled over, swinging his legs over the edge of the bed. "Get my chair for me?" he asked.

Poochie got Ray's chair, while at the same time telling him how he didn't miss much at dinner.

"What's up, ya'll?" 1-Punch asked. He was standing with Joe-Joe. They both looked as if they needed something to do.

"What's up?" Ray responded to them.

"I was just tellin' the homie that dinner was some garbage."

"Yeah, it was," Joe-Joe agreed.

1-Punch walked around Joe-Joe, making a wide circle. "Ain't no such thing as garbage to you, fat boy," he teased Joe-Joe. "You'll eat anything."

Poochie laughed at how 1-Punch leaned backwards when he said that to Joe-Joe.

"Excuse me, dawg." Ray slid into his wheelchair and made it over to the bathrooms. He wanted to wash up. Poochie was standing at his bunk with some goodies.

"I got noodles, cookies, cakes, ummm...I got some more stuff in my bag if you want somethin' else."

Ray smiled. He was a little hungry. "Let me get one of those noodles and some cookies. I'll get you back when we go to the store."

Poochie gestured him off with a wave. "Don't trip, dawg. We're homies, Ray!"

"I appreciate it, man. Look," Ray began with a grunt. "After I eat, I'mma lie back down. I don't mean anything by it. I just got a few things on my mind and I'm still a little tired."

The expression on Poochie's face said that he understood. "Just call me if you need me, all right? I'll be standin' close by so I can keep my eye on you while you rest. As for the soup," he said, pointing at the hot water dispenser, "I got you."

Poochie made the soup for Ray, although Ray insisted he could do it himself. After Poochie brought Ray the bowl, he left him to himself and Ray was grateful. He wanted to be alone. He ate his meal in peace, sitting and taking in the scenery around him. It was evening and the guys in the unit were playing cards, checkers, chess, and hanging out in groups conversing. He could tell that the majority of the guys in the groups were gangbangers by the way they carried themselves.

That walk, that talk, that swagger...yeah, they're bangin', he thought.

For the rest of the night, Ray lay in his bunk and let

his thoughts focus on Momma Wilson, Big Mack, and Trena. It was crazy how everything took a turn for the worse, he thought. He was worried about Momma Wilson and wished he could be there to support her. He had asked Poochie earlier about making a telephone call, and Poochie told him that they were only allowed to make calls through the counselor.

"Steele is tough," Poochie told him. "He's been on us hard lately."

Ray saw right then that it was in his best interests to get on Counselor Steele's good side. Especially since he knew that the only way he'd get to talk to Momma Wilson and Trena was through Steele. His mind drifted as he pondered whether Trena would really wait on him until he got out.

A girl that pretty... he thought, *chances are slim.*

Somehow, though, he believed that anything was possible, so he vowed not to count her out. He really wanted her to stay down for him.

The streets were talking and Ray knew it. He couldn't keep his mind from wondering what was being said. Big Mack had a name for himself, while Ray and C-Dog were best friends. All of the right components were in play for 'hood gossip. But this was real life to him, and all the things that had happened affected him greatly. Big Mack had been his mentor, his teacher...his family. After his mother was murdered, all that was left in his life to sustain him was Big Mack and Momma Wilson. *Man,* he thought, *the streets done taken away so much from me.*

His mind wandered until he heard the unit officer say, "Lights out," and everyone was sent to their respective bunks. Ray lay in the dark, contemplating his life, a life that had been scarred with bullets, murder, and now, incarceration.

Chapter Ten

For Ray, getting comfortable in his new environment was hard to do. His first few days were spent experiencing firsthand what Fred C. Nelles was all about. He could tell it was designed not only to keep young troublemakers off the streets, but it also incorporated a system that taught them responsibility and to be respectful toward authority. These were two things that he had no problem with. Big Mack had always taught him that if he respected the game, the game would respect him. Momma Wilson taught him to respect himself, life, and his elders. And both Big Mack and Momma Wilson taught him how to become responsible. From what he saw, a lot of the young men at Nelles had never been taught anything. Anything, that is, except for gangbangin'. Nelles had school for those who needed it, and those who had already gotten their GEDs were provided jobs. Monday through Friday from eight-thirty to four, everyone in the unit was busy doing something.

Counselor Steele called Ray into his office, located just inside the dormitory, a week after he arrived. Steele informed Ray that he would be meeting with him later for his first one-on-one discussion. He also informed Ray that his files indicated that he needed to attend classes, and recommended that he pursue his GED before he got out.

"You'd be surprised how much good it'll do you," Steele encouraged Ray.

Physical exercise was also stressed at Nelles. Groups would be taken outside to perform various strenuous exercises. Pull ups, push-ups, stretches, and running were done every day. They also had weights, which were used regularly. Some of the young guys walking around were so muscular that they looked like they were doing time in state prison. Buff was one of them, and

Ray noticed quickly that everyone seemed to stay out of his way. Everyone else seemed to have something to do, while Ray was enjoying the idle medical status he was given for his injuries, which prevented him from doing almost everything.

* * *

Ray had been at Nelles a full week and visiting had come and gone with a no-show from Momma Wilson and Trena. During the week he had seen Counselor Steele once and had asked him for a telephone call, but he was denied.

"Man, that Steele is somethin' else. I haven't talked to my mom since I've been here and I asked him for a call but he said, 'Not right now.' Man, that dude…"

"L'il Ray, you got to chill out," Poochie suggested. "He's gonna let you use the phone, but not if he feels like you're pressin' him into doin' it."

Ray gave off a healthy chuckle. "Tsk! Pressin'! Man, I haven't pressed no one. All I did was tell him that I needed to use the phone to holla at someone and he said, 'Not right now.' He didn't even ask me who I was try'nah call."

Poochie laughed, looking over his shoulder as if looking for someone. "Man, that's just Steele for you. But, for the most part, he's cool when it comes to helpin' us. Just be cool, homie."

Ray looked at him without any expression. Hesitantly, he said, "Yeah, I guess you're right. I guess I'm kind of anxious to talk to my mom, that's all. But what's up with all this tension goin' on around here between the Blacks and the Mexicans?" Ray looked around the unit at everyone's seating arraignments.

Poochie shrugged in a confused manner. "I don't know, dawg. I guess it's just somethin' in the air."

Ray nodded and licked his lips. "Yeah, but what

started it?" he inquired inquisitively. He had never witnessed anything like this before, the way each group was sectioned off by race, giving each other cold stares, the way they whispered in each other's ears and nodded in each other's direction. Ray looked around at everything that was transpiring and just as he did, he saw the inevitable. A tall, slim black guy who wore his standard blue shirt and denim jeans sagging below his buttocks, walked past a Mexican and White guy who were talking. They exchanged heartless stares with frowns on their faces, trying to be mean, mugging at each other. They never said a word, nor budged to give the other room to pass. Ray was in disbelief. Even though he heard it on the streets, it seemed like it was an ongoing beef that he had never seen with his own two eyes.

"Man, I don't even know how it started up in here. I heard that it was handed down through generations of 14th Streets to the Tiny Dukes or something like that. Maybe it come from the Mafia and everybody's just ridin' on their coattails. Whatever it is, you can believe it's some penitentiary stuff that doesn't make any sense."

Seeing how it was being played out before his very eyes was another thing. Ray shook his head. "Yeah, you're probably right. It probably don't make any sense."

The two groups were totally segregated in everything. There were Blacks-only tables and a Mexican-only table, even though both tables were identical in size and shape. The same thing occurred in the chow hall. Both groups ate separately and gathered separately in everything they did. The looks that Ray had seen the two groups give each other were nothing less than menacing. The whole thing reminded him of a scene from *Mississippi Burning*, and the way Blacks and Whites acted and treated each other in the sixties. And there he was, just watching the show.

Ray was on his way back from getting his daily checkup from Medical when he was met by Poochie, 1-Punch, and Joe-Joe. To him they looked as though they had just gotten off a hard day's work.

"What's up, young G?" 1-Punch said, flashing a smile.

"Nothin' much," Ray replied. He couldn't put his finger on it, but for some strange reason he really didn't like how people attributed status to a person after something tragic had happened, or when they had done something outright stupid. *But that's how the streets are*, he thought, reminiscing about what Big Mack use to say to him.

"Let me get that."

Ray looked up. "You don't have to, dawg. I know ya'll just finished workin' out."

"Where you comin' from?" Poochie got behind Ray's wheelchair and began to push him back to their housing unit, taking the strain off of Ray's arms. The wheelchair was giving him problems due to the fact he had to exert a lot of energy to wheel himself around. But, he had to admit that it was a much needed workout. Ray knew that he wasn't the strongest fish in the pond.

"Where you comin' from?' Joe-Joe asked with sweat beading off his forehead.

Ray looked up at him. "Medical," he responded. "They've been runnin' tests and stuff. The doctor wants to make sure the swellin' is goin' down in my back."

"Yeah," 1-Punch cut in. "You got a few bullets lodged in ya' spine, huh?"

"Naw, just one. Close to my spine, but not lodged in it."

All four entered the building and were welcomed in the after-work, after-school rush. 1-Punch and Joe-Joe expressed their plans to get in the shower and Poochie said he was on his way to do the same after he pushed Ray to his bunk.

"Thanks," Ray told him.

"No problem, homie."

Just then the officer made his way toward Ray.

"James Ray Turner?"

"Yeah."

"Steele wants to see you in his office."

Poochie looked at Ray and smiled. "One-on-one."

"I'm on my way," Ray responded to the officer. "Hey, man, I'll see you later," he told Poochie and wheeled himself in the direction of Counselor Steele's office, where he found the door wide open. Ray knocked on the open door.

Steele looked up from his desk. "Come on in, Turner," he said, just hanging up the telephone.

Ray did as he was told. He pulled his chair into the office and sat before a serious-faced man who looked like he was going to be all about business. "Close the door."

Ray looked a little hesitant. He didn't want anyone to think that he was in Steele's office talking about things he had no business talking about.

"Close it, son. I make everybody do it," Steele assured him. "Plus, there isn't anything that goes on around here that I don't already know about, anyways."

Ray backed his wheelchair up and closed the door.

"Okay," Steele said, leaning back in his chair. "So, what's your story?"

Ray was confused, but he tried not to show any signs of it. "What do you mean?"

Steele closed his eyes and slowly rotated his neck to release the tension. He sighed. "I mean, what are you doin' here? What are you trying to accomplish? What do you want out of life? Your story?"

Ray didn't know where all these questions were leading, so he just answered the question that seemed the most obvious to him. "I'm here because my P.O. violated my probation."

Steele shook his head with a grimace. "I see that! Remember, I got your file sittin' right here in front of me. What I'm askin' you, though, your file can't answer."

Ray was still confused and this time he let it show. "Man, I don't know what you mean then. You keep askin' me what am I here for, but you already know what I'm here for!"

Steele steepled his fingers and placed them to his mouth. He stared at Ray. Calm and poised, like he had done this a million times before, Counselor Steele leaned his wide frame forward and rested his thick forearms on his desk. "What do you claim, Turner?"

Ray cocked his head to the side and looked as if he were puzzled by the man. "What do I claim?"

Still keeping his composure, Steele clarified his question. "Yes. What set you claimin'? Blood, Crip? I know you're no Black Mexican or it would've been in your files. So, what is it?"

Ray laughed out loud. "Man, I don't bang," he answered calmly.

"What? Am I mistaken, or aren't you from the same neighborhood as Joseph Calhoun and Floater Warhop?"

Ray shrugged his shoulders. "Yeah, and?"

"Aren't they Bloods?"

Ray sighed. "I don't be goin' around askin' people what they are. I know we're from the same neighborhood. You say you know everything that goes on around here, so if you say they're Bloods I guess you're right."

"Well, there it is! I saw you chillin' with them and..."

"Man, look," Ray interjected. "Everybody that lives in the 'hood doesn't bang. I already told you and everybody else that asked me about it that I don't bang. Yeah, they're from the same 'hood as me, but I'm about my money, and they do what they do."

Steele Looked at Ray for a moment, studying him, without saying a word. Then his shoulders relaxed. Looking satisfied, like he had grasped a jewel of information, he leaned back in his chair. "I called Mrs.

Wilson and talked with her for a while. She told me you were never into gangs, but I know how kids can hide a lot from their parents. I've seen it a million times before. Parents think their little boy's an angel, but the whole time he's a gangsta Crip wanted for a dozen or more drive-bys."

Ray heard the man, but all that registered in his mind was Momma Wilson's name. "When did you talk to her?"

"Oh, the day before yesterday," Steele confessed, looking to the ceiling as if he were in deep thought. "She told me she would be here to see you this weekend, too."

That's what he needed to hear. He needed to know that she was okay. Ray relaxed and let his body sink into his chair.

"So, Turner, you're not into gangs, you're into money. What's this deal about gettin' shot then?"

"Man, like I told the other police, I don't know who shot me."

Now it was Steele's turn to share a slight laugh. "Son, I'm not askin' you who shot you. I'm askin' you what part of the game is worth gettin' shot over?"

This question caught Ray off guard. "I don't know..."

Steele shook his head, staring at Ray. "Boy, if you say that you don't know what I mean one more time..." Steele showed frustration for the first time. "My question again is, what part of the game was worth gettin' shot over? You said you're about money, right? Well, what... part...was...worth...it?"

Ray thought for a moment about what Counselor Steele was asking. He didn't know how to answer, so he said, "Man, it comes with it!"

Steele didn't show any expression at all. "Okay. Well, was it worth it?"

Ray shrugged. "Like I said, this is all a part of the game. But as long as there are players, the game don't stop."

Steele shook his head again in disbelief. "It doesn't stop, huh?" He laughed at what he had heard. "You know, I talked to Mrs. Wilson, like I said, and she told me that your brother was killed along with another lady. Your police report say it was all behind a drug deal gone bad. So, I'm askin' you if it was worth it. And you're tellin' me that it comes along with the game like you've accepted this for what it is. Can you honestly say two human lives, and you sittin' here with three bullet wounds in your body that left you in this wheelchair, was worth it?"

Ray knew what Steele was trying to say and he just dropped his head.

"Mrs. Wilson told me she's been prayin' that you use this time to change for the better. She told me you're the only son, the only family she has left. Ray," Counselor Steele paused. He leaned forward on his desk again and spoke in a low, caring tone. "Son, ask yourself: What am I doin' here? What am I tryin' to accomplish and what do I want out of life? Ask yourself this, because until you answer these questions for yourself, you're nothin' more than a person with no purpose in life. It doesn't matter if you've banged or not. What matters the most is what you do from this point forward. Think about it, son."

A correctional officer tapped three times on the door, signaling to Counselor Steele that it was count time.

"Look, Turner," Steele continued. "I've got close to a hundred and twenty kids in this unit and I try to have one-on-ones with them once a month. This just ain't routine with me as far as what my job requires. This here," he said, poking his index finger on the desk, "this is personal. So if you ever have any questions or need someone to talk to, my door is always open. You've survived somethin' that many kids haven't. Think about all of that and recognize a blessing for what it is."

Ray heard the man and his words made a lot of

sense. He didn't know why the counselor showed so much concern, but he couldn't deny the truth. It wasn't worth it.

Counselor Steele dismissed Ray and he made it out of the office just as the officer hollered, "Count time!"

1-Punch was on his way out of the shower, walking with his towel around his neck. He pushed his chest out and shoulders back as he bowed his arms, giving off his best impression of Counselor Steele. "Yo'! L'il Ray!"

Ray stopped and looked toward him.

1-Punch deepened his voice. "Boy, what do you want out of life?" The joke seemed to tickle 1-Punch to the bone.

Ray didn't laugh. To him, Steele's three questions were deserving of some honest consideration. Shaking his head, he rolled on toward his bunk. On his way, he felt an awkward feeling and noticed a small group of men gathered by a bunk, staring at him. Mexicans! Ray stopped his wheelchair and looked back, not knowing why he even stopped to acknowledge them. Maybe it was because he didn't know why they were staring at him like they were. Whatever the reason was, he let them know that he had seen them.

"You lost somethin'?"

Ray turned in his seat kind of startled. It was Buff.

"Man, those *esses* over there…what they lookin' at?"

Buff looked in the direction that Ray was referring to and said, "Man, that's just Javier and some of his homeboys. They're from the Tiny Dukes in Riverside. I used to go to school with him. Don't trip on him. He just wants attention," Buff assured as he pushed Ray to his bunk.

Chapter Eleven

Ray had gotten word that he was getting a visit, and couldn't wait until they started letting visitors into the room. When the time came, he moved his wheelchair so fast that he swore he heard the rubber on the wheels make a screeching sound on the unit's floor.

"There goes my baby," the visitor said, greeting him with a hug.

Ray was all smiles. "Hey, Momma, I thought you forgot about me."

Momma Wilson smiled. "How could I, son, how could I?"

To him, Momma Wilson looked a little worn down. *Understandable, considering everything she's been through*, he thought. He pulled his wheelchair in front of her as she sat down on a dark blue, durable plastic chair. The spacious, cream colored, tiled room had seat-sized plastic tables to match the chairs that separated the visitor from the ward. Microwaves were placed against the wall next to the officers' podium, and the officers' station overlooked the visiting room.

This is nice compared to D-unit, Ray thought.

"So, how is it going for you up in there?"

"Momma," Ray shrugged, "it's been hard bein' away from you. I can't stop worryin' about if you're all right."

Momma Wilson smiled at the thought. It seemed to bring light and life to her old soul. "I thought you'd be thinking about Trena and wouldn't have time for thinking about little old me," she said, brushing the palm of her hand across his cheek.

"No one comes before you, Momma," Ray assured her with finality.

Ray and Momma Wilson talked as he told her all about Fred C. Nelles. He told her how Floater Warhop and

Joe-Joe Calhoun were both there with him.

"Little chubby Joseph? Deacon Calhoun's grandson?"

Ray smiled. "Yes, ma'am."

Momma Wilson just shook her head. "You boys just grew up so fast. I remember when he was a little baby. The boy's momma dressed him up in all black and put shoe polish all over his face for Halloween. They told me he was supposed to be a burglar, but his little round butt looked like a bowling ball to me. He knocked on my door and I just wanted to take him in my arms and bowl him back down my sidewalk."

Ray started laughing at how animated Momma Wilson was, swinging her arm as if she had just thrown a bowling ball.

"So, son," she continued, "how have you been?"

He knew she was referring to his wounds. "I've been fine, Momma. They send me to the doctor almost every day."

Momma Wilson nodded her head in relief upon hearing that he was getting good care. "Trena told me to tell you she wrote you. She couldn't make it up here with me. Her dad just hasn't come around yet."

Ray knew that something was wrong. Momma Wilson could tell that this news got him down by the expression on his face.

She lifted his chin. "Don't worry, baby. He'll see. They'll all see. I got the whole church praying with me, baby, and the devil won't get both my boys."

When she said this, Ray lifted his eyes to meet hers. "Momma, don't say that. The devil doesn't have Big Mack."

Momma Wilson smiled. "Baby, God has Macarthur, but it was the devil's work that made it happen." Then she leaned across the table and took Ray's hand into hers. "Ray, the devil is in those streets and in those people out there. I want you to look and look good! See, the devil will make all of it look good to you. The fast money, the nice cars, the girls. But when you look at all these things real good, you'll see it's all an illusion. It's not what it seems to be. What he's offering you leads to death."

Ray listened and was moved by the compassion in her voice.

"Ray, God has placed you in here for a reason, for you to take a good look at your life. They wanted to send Macarthur to one of these places when he was around your age, and sometimes I wish they had done it. Sometimes it's good for a person to step to the side and take some time out just to look at himself. That counselor, umm…Mr. Steele… called me and he asked me a bunch of questions. Ray, baby, I was honest with him and I hope you're not disappointed with me."

This caught him off guard. "Momma, I could never be disappointed…"

"I know, I know," Momma Wilson continued with assurance in her voice. "I just know how people can mean good and say something that causes more harm. I only want the best for you, son. I want you to start anew and come out of here refreshed."

Ray was moved and he wanted to make her proud of him. "But what do I do? I don't know what to do," he questioned sincerely.

Momma Wilson rubbed her hands across his and held them tightly. "Ray, turn to the Lord. Get closer to God and ask Him to give you the wisdom, knowledge, and strength to change. Do this, and you'll make your first step toward a new life. All you have to do is take the first step."

If anyone else had said this to him, the words would have fallen on deaf ears. But because he knew that Momma Wilson would always tell him what was best for him, he tried to listen.

For the rest of the visit Ray sat and enjoyed his time with Momma Wilson. Their conversation seemed to be more intimate than ever before. He couldn't help but think about how tragedy pulled families together.

When the end of visiting hours came, Ray thought it had come too soon. Momma Wilson expressed her goodbyes and said she was going to put some money on his commissary account, even though he insisted that he was fine. Seeing she would hear nothing of it, he surrendered and told her he would give her a call when she got home, if his counselor would allow him to.

"I'll ask Counselor Steele when I get in," he explained. "I know I should be good for a call by now."

Momma Wilson made her way out of the visiting room and Ray called out to her. "Momma, tell Trena that when I get her letter I'mma write her straight back."

* * *

"Yo', Counselor Steele." Ray wheeled himself into the dorm, fresh off his visit, riding on cloud nine.

Counselor Steele was sitting in his office, just finishing a conversation with a young guy who favored Ashton Kutcher. "Yeah, come on in, Turner," Steele said, followed by a hand gesture.

"Man, look," Ray began. "I know we gotta come through you, so I wanted to know if you'd allow me to make a call to make sure my mom gets home all right?"

Steele knew that Ray had just come off his visit. Without looking up, he answered, "See me in an hour."

Cool! Ray thought, spinning around in his chair and heading in the direction of his bunk.

Count time was in twenty minutes, so he decided to lie down on his bunk until then. Poochie, Joe-Joe, 1-Punch, and Buff were all playing spades at a table and everyone else around was engaged in recreation activities, standing around talking, joking, or playing other games. The officers in the unit had to occasionally stop some of the guys from horseplaying. Horseplaying was never tolerated because it resembled violence, and that was something Ray knew the administration wanted to break the guys from doing.

The officers called count time and made their rounds, counting each ward one by one. As they came to the end of each row, they congregated, checking to see if each one had the same count.

Ray chilled out, letting his mind drift back to the conversation he'd had earlier with Momma Wilson. *She really needs me to change,* he thought. *But I can't just walk away after C-Dog killed Big Mack and tried to kill me. What would people say when I get back out there try'nah get money? I'mma die a thug,* he rationalized. That was how he saw himself.

When an hour had passed, he made his way back to Counselor Steele's office and, just like Steele had promised, Ray made his call.

The phone rang. There was no answer. Ray allowed the phone to continue to ring, but still there was no answer. *Where could she be?* he thought.

"Look, Turner, I'm on my way home right now, but if you want to try back tomorrow, I'll be in. I'll let you try again then. Sometime around lunch will be cool."

Ray was confused. "All right," he said, still letting the phone ring.

"Don't look so down, Turner," Steele said, noticing the disturbed look on Ray's face. "She just probably stopped by one of her friends' houses before goin' home."

"Friends' houses?" Ray exclaimed. "Momma Wilson don't go nowhere besides Bible Study, Sunday school, and church. Naw, Mr. Steele, somethin's wrong," Ray said, shaking his head.

"Son," Steele said after a long pause. "Ain't nothin' gonna happen to Mrs. Wilson. Trust me, she's okay. Now, if you want me to, I'll call her and let her know to be expectin' your call tomorrow."

Ray nodded his head as he handed the telephone back to Steele. *Dang, Momma!* he thought.

* * *

That night as Ray lay under his covers, he still felt the weight of worry on his heart and mind. Although Momma Wilson had spoken in an upbeat spirit to him, she just didn't look the same. Her eyes looked swollen, like she had been crying.

She looks weak, he thought.

Now, as everyone tossed in their bunks and the lights were dimmed, Ray found himself concerned for the only family he had left in his life. He knew without Momma Wilson things wouldn't be the same. It would be too much to lose the two people he loved so much in such a short period of time. Slowly, fearful thoughts started settling in.

What if somethin' has happened to Momma Wilson? What if she's had a car accident and no one knows where she's at? What if C-Dog...I'll kill him, so help me, Ray rationalized. "Momma Wilson, where are you?" he mumbled as he slowly turned onto his side and closed his eyes. "Lord," he began in an unsure voice. "Ahhh, it's me, Ray. Man, I know I haven't got at'chu much lately. But I'm callin' you because I'm worried about Momma Wilson. Now see, I know I'm what'chu call a sinner and I'm not even sure if you wanna talk to me right now. But, look, you're the only one I know who can help. Momma Wilson loves you and she's always good to you. She's hurtin' right now and I'm responsible for some of it. Can you please find her and make sure she's all right? If you do, I'll make a promise wit'chu." Ray hesitated a few seconds because he wasn't the type to give his word unless he was going to keep it. "Man, if you look out for Momma Wilson until I get out, I'll try hard to be better, like she asked me to. But

I'm gonna need your help because that dude C-Dog done messed up my life. Keepin' it real, I do owe you one because you could've let me die and you didn't, so good lookin' out. Plus, I know Momma Wilson is gonna need me to take care of her when I get out and if I'm in them streets, it'll only stress her even more. She's gettin' old and Mack is gone now, so all she's got is me."

Ray didn't understand why it was happening, but tears welled up in the corners of his eyes. He wiped at the tears that ran down the side of his face. He sniffled. "God, just keep her safe. You do your part and I promise to do mine. You can ask Big Mack, he'll tell you. I keep my word! Oh, yeah. If it's not a problem, if you ask him about me could you please tell him I love him? Good lookin' out God. One love. Amen."

Ray finished his prayer and rolled back onto his back. In his mind he figured that nothing could go wrong if a person had to call on God for help.

Chapter Twelve

Ray was sitting on his bunk drying off his feet, which was like a full time job in itself. *Man!* Ray thought as he felt the tightness in his back. Even though he was moving a little bit better than he had been, he knew that he was still miles away from where he wanted to be physically. It still took almost thirty minutes for him to dry off well, put on some lotion, and struggle into his socks and pants. When he finished that routine, he sat back on his bunk, wiped the sweat from his forehead and finally relaxed.

Ever since he'd awakened, he'd had the prayer he'd said the night before on his mind, as well as the promise he'd made. He couldn't wait until lunchtime to see Counselor Steele for that call. It was Sunday, and although Poochie told him that Steele didn't work on Sundays, Ray hoped that the counselor would keep his word. Now, finally dressed and full from a hefty brunch of eggs and pancakes, Ray set out to find something to occupy his time.

"Poochie," Ray called out to his neighborhood friend. Ray had come to really appreciate Floater for the help he always offered, especially since the incident with C-Dog had quietly created a phobia in Ray toward so-called homeboys.

"What's up, L'il Ray?" Poochie dropped what he was doing and hurried to see what his friend wanted.

"Yo', you don't have nothin' to read over there, do you?"

"Naw," Poochie said, shaking his head. "All I got is my school stuff. You know, I'm in that GED class, so I just study that."

Ray nodded.

"But if you want somethin' like a novel or somethin', there's a bookrack over there against the wall."

Ray looked over to where Poochie was pointing and saw the rack of books. "Good lookin' out."

Poochie really didn't mind helping out. "You want me to push you over there?"

"Naw, I got it," Ray smiled.

The bookrack was filled to capacity. There were six shelves that sat on wheels that reminded him of something that came off a grocery basket. The books were of various categories from romance, mystery, action, suspense, thriller, to motivational. Ray sat for a minute, mesmerized by all of the titles, hoping to find something that interested him.

"Yo', Ray," came a voice behind him. It was 1-Punch. "Check out those cowboy books. They be killin' up some stuff in there. Or those romantic ones be havin' all types of sex stuff in 'em, too."

Ray nodded, acknowledging that he'd heard him. *That dude is off the chain*, Ray thought. He returned his attention to the bookshelves and continued to search. *Murder mysteries and science fiction, hmmmm*, he thought. Ray moved and shuffled the books around, trying to see if anything good was hidden somewhere in the bunch. When he did this, a small book fell onto the floor. When he reached to pick it up, he noticed what it was. Shrugging his shoulders, he placed it back on the cart. Reaching for a mystery, he dropped the book in his lap and began to wheel himself back to his bunk, but then he stopped as the thought of Momma Wilson crossed his mind. Ray sat for a moment in the middle of the aisle, and then he turned around and went to retrieve the small book he had placed back on the shelf. He tucked it underneath his mystery novel and returned to his bunk. *This will do,* he thought.

Following their normal routine, everyone in the housing unit congregated in their groups and indulged in small talk. Ray noticed Counselor Steele walk into the unit and go straight to his office, warding off a few guys who ran up to him asking a lot of questions. There was no need for Ray to bother Steele, because he knew that the counselor told him to come see him after lunch. Ray decided to wait until then. He lay back on his bunk and opened the little book first to keep him occupied until then.

"Yo', Ray!"

Without looking, he knew who it was: 1-Punch.

"What's up?" Ray said.

"Man, what the... What are you readin', gangsta?"

He was really beginning to get tired of 1-Punch.

"What does it look like?" Ray snapped with a little frustration in his voice.

1-Punch was standing with a small group of young men next to a table. Ray's question seemed to catch him off guard. "It looks like one of those l'il Bibles," he giggled.

"Man, you smart," Ray replied in a voice that said, "You just won a brand new car!"

Ray could tell that 1-Punch had caught his drift.

"Aye, my bad kill'ah. I was just askin'."

After 1-Punch had finished, Ray shook his head and returned his attention on the pocket-sized book, which fell open on the book of Matthew. He began to read. When his mother died, he remembered having nightmares and Momma Wilson would read him stories from the Bible so he would fall asleep. There was something about the stories and his remembrances of them that had caused him to pick up the book.

He noticed that the book was broken into chapters, and the chapters were sectioned off into little parables and stories. Each one had a heading over the top of it. "Jesus feeds five thousand," he read under his breath. "I got to read this!"

Just as he began to get into the story, Ray felt someone staring at him. He looked over and saw who it was. There was a Mexican guy about his age, sitting on his bunk about three rows away, looking directly at him. He had seen him before, but never really paid any attention to him, until now.

"What's up, holmes?" Ray asked him.

The young man looked at Ray and smiled. "Ahh, my bad," he replied, shaking his head. "I didn't mean to stare. I was just curious to know what you were readin'," he added with a slight accent.

"This is crazy!" Ray mumbled, setting the book down. "Hasn't anyone ever seen somebody read the Bible around here?" he asked in a serious tone, trying to keep his cool.

"Naw, holmes. I was just wonderin'," he said in his broken English. "I read the Bible a lot, too, and it's rare you see people readin' them around here."

Ray saw that the guy didn't mean him any harm. "Yeah, ahh...I'm readin' a book by some dude named Matthew."

The Mexican guy smiled. "He was a disciple of Jesus."

Ray nodded. "Yeah, and he wrote somethin' about Jesus feedin' five thousand people."

The Mexican guy smiled at Ray and said, "If you get a chance, check out the next story where Peter walks on water."

Ray laughed. *Walks on water!* he thought. "I gotta read that!"

The Mexican guy nodded. "I gotta get ready for service."

Ray watched as he grabbed a few books from his bunk and noticed instantly a Bible in his hand.

"Oh yeah! My name is José."

Ray smiled. "They call me L'il Ray."

"Nice to meet you, Ray," José said, still smiling.

That dude is really happy, Ray thought. *All this tension goin' on around here between the Mexicans and us, and he's smilin'.* Ray shook his head. *First time for everything.*

Ray lay in his bunk and read in a low pitch, letting the story intrigue, teach, and confuse him all at the same time. *Man,* Ray thought, trying to understand what he was reading. "When the disciples saw Him walking on the sea, they were terrified ... Peter said to Him, Lord, if it is you ... get out of the boat..." *Man this is crazy,* he thought.

By the time lunch came around, he was good and hungry. He made his way to the chow hall with the rest of the guys, escorted by correctional officers in a single-file line. When he made it back from eating, it didn't seem like it was soon enough. He was anxious to call Momma Wilson.

Counselor Steele was waiting on him as he wheeled himself through the door. "You got ten minutes, Turner," Steele said without looking up.

"But..."

Counselor Steele turned the telephone toward him and allowed him to dial the number. There was an answer on the first ring.

"Hello?"

Ray's heartbeat slowed as he heard her voice. "Momma, where have you been? I've been try'nah call. Yesterday when you left I thought somethin' happened to you. You weren't home and I got worried." Ray continued rambling, telling her about his worries.

Momma Wilson laughed. "Boy, you sound like my husband. I'm all right. When I left you I decided to stop by Doctor McBride's office so he could take all my vitals."

"Thank you, man," Ray whispered, looking up at the ceiling. "Well, what did he say?"

"Well, after I got him to focus on my vitals and not on my pretty looks, he said I was in good health. You know, Dr. McBride and I went to school together in the sixties. He thinks I didn't know he had a crush on me," she said playfully.

Ray laughed out loud. Just hearing Momma Wilson's voice was enough to ease his nerves, and hearing that she was in good health was a plus. Even though Ray only had ten minutes, he used every one of them to tell her how he felt. "Momma, you know last night after I couldn't get in touch with you I got worried and started to pray and asked God to watch after you."

"Oh baby," she began, "you don't have to worry about me."

"Momma, I do, because you're the only one I have left in my life. All we have is each other, so I made a promise to God that if He made sure you was all right, I'll try to do better. I told Him that Big Mack's gone and I'm the only one who can look after you. Momma, I even read the Bible because...because I don't know what I'd do if I lost you, too."

Momma Wilson paused. She cleared her throat. "My goodness," she said, surprised. She knew that Ray had been through a lot, but this was something she was not expecting. "Baby, no matter what happens to me, God is going to always make sure you're all right. He knows that we need each other, but don't just make a promise to Him that you'll try to do better when you're scared and worried about me. Make it because that's what you really want to do. You hear me?"

"Yes, ma'am."

"Baby, I'm saying this because after I left yesterday I thought about you and the things you and Macarthur used to do, and it hurt me to think that when you come home you might try to do the same old things. Do you remember that boy that ya'll used to shoot dice with on the corner? I believe his name was Little Donald, or something like that?"

Ray thought about the last time he encountered Little Donald on his birthday. "Yeah, I remember him."

"Well, they found his body in a canal. The news

said somebody chopped off his arms and legs."

Ray immediately shook his head in disbelief. *L'il Donald!* he thought, reminiscing about the last time he saw him, when he pulled his pistol on him when they were shooting dice. "Is that right?"

"Yeah," she continued, "that's why I pray for you every night. The devil is trying to get everybody, but baby, I won't let him have you, too."

Ray looked at Counselor Steele. "He's not gonna get me, Momma."

"I know, I know baby, but don't stop reading your Bible. And whenever you're discouraged or feeling down, or just worried and feeling scared, pick it up and read Psalm 91, because it'll give you a sense of protection and peace in more ways than one."

Ray smiled and glanced at Steele again. "I will."

Just then Counselor Steele gave him that look that said his time was up.

"Momma, I love you and I gotta go now."

"Okay. Oh! Trena told me to tell you hi and that she misses you."

Ray was really on cloud nine now. "Tell her I said the same."

"Okay, I'll talk to you later, baby."

Ray hung up the telephone. He thanked Counselor Steele, who gave him an awkward look. But Ray was so happy about hearing his mother's voice that he didn't even bother to pay it any attention. He was too busy feeling good.

* * *

"Ray."

He was lying down reading a magazine when he heard his name being called. He looked over and saw who it was. "Hey, what's up José?"

José smiled. "So, what you think?"

Ray was confused about what he was referring to. "What I think about what?"

He watched as José sat down on his bunk to get comfortable.

"Matthew," he answered.

"Matthew? Ooh, yeah! Man..." Ray leaned on one elbow and turned toward José. "It was cool, but I just couldn't get past a few things."

"Like what?"

Ray wiggled in his bunk. "Well, for one, how Jesus feed five thousand people with five loaves of bread and two fish. Now, if my calculations are correct, there's probably twenty slices of bread in a loaf, not includin' the ends. So that's a hundred slices of bread. As for the fish, man, they must've grounded that stuff up like tuna in a can."

José couldn't help but laugh at Ray's humor. "So what did you think about Peter?"

"Hold on," he continued. "After that came the story where Jesus and Peter started walkin' on water. On water! Come on, José! I've seen dudes high off water but never walkin' on top of it. What's up with that?"

José was intrigued by Ray's inquisitiveness. He leaned forward and said, "You have to understand that a lot of stories in the Bible hold a jewel. A deeper meanin', and these meanin's can help us have a better understanding about life and ourselves when we know how they relate to us."

Ray thought that José sounded really smart. "Well, tell me the meanin' of these stories."

"Okay. For one, you got to slow down, Ray," José said with his usual smile. "Now, which one would you like me to explain first? That's a lot of scripture to cover, and I would hate it if you took too much at once."

Ray smiled at José. "Man, just tell me what it means when it says they walked on water," he said with a chuckle.

"I've seen leaves and sticks float on water, but I ain't ever seen anyone walk on it!"

José rocked back and forth with his hands clasped together. He slowly exhaled. "Ray...there's a story in the Bible about how the children of Israel complained to Moses because they were thirsty. Moses cried out to the Lord because he didn't know what to do. The Lord instructed him to use his rod to strike a rock and water would come gushin' out of it for the people to drink."

Anxiously, Ray interjected, "But what does that have to do with him..."

"Hold on, hold on," José said with a hand gesture. "This water that they talk about in the Bible is *seambolic* of the spirit. See..."

Ray had a confused look on his face. "*Seambolic?*" Ray questioned. "What does that mean?"

José paused. "It's somethin' that...that relates to somethin' else. Like a seambol for it."

Ray smiled. "Oh, you mean symbolic?"

"Yeah, yeah, Ray, that's what I meant. Seam-bol-ic! Anyways, when Jesus walked on water it's like in the midst of His circumstances the Holy Spirit sustained Him."

"Oooooh," Ray said, nodding his head. "But what circumstances?"

José smiled and shook his head. "I figured you'd ask me that. See, Jesus knew that he was facing death and at times his Spirit was disturbed. But because he loved us so much he refused to waver. And because he walked in the Spirit of love, and moved by the same Spirit, those things sustained him from sinking. They sustained Peter when he took his eyes off his circumstances, and put them back on Jesus." José hesitated. "Ray, if you accept Christ as your Lord and Savior, the Holy Spirit will sustain you, too. I see you sittin' in that wheelchair so I know somethin' bad happened to you. I also know it's easy for us to fall back to our old ways once we get out of here."

Ray listened and watched as the smile on José's face vanished.

José continued. "But what if you don't make it next time? What if...if you die? How many people are you gonna leave behind that need you? Think about it, because you don't have to fall victim to your circumstances like Peter. The Holy Spirit will raise the standard in your life that sustains you." He stood and began to walk away. "You don't have to sink back into your old ways, Ray, or fall victim to the circumstances around you."

Ray sat quietly, pondering everything José had said. The interpretation that José had given him of Jesus and Peter walking on water was given in such a way that he would've never seen otherwise. He watched José walk toward his bunk area and noticed that his smile did not return. "Hey, is that stuff true, what you just said?"

José turned around and finally smiled. "You know, God reveals things to us, sometimes in different ways. You could read a story and God could give you a revelation from that story that I wouldn't have seen. But in the end, the only important question about the message is whether you believe the Holy Spirit can sustain you in the midst of your circumstances."

Ray nodded his head. He understood.

José walked back toward Ray's bunk and the two of them talked for a while longer, lost in their conversation. Both made themselves a little more familiar with each other, sharing a lot of personal information. Ray found out that José was locked up for possession of firearms. He was in a car with some of his friends and they had guns in the car. The police pulled them over just before they were about to do something stupid. He was fourteen at the time, and now he was almost seventeen.

"Yeah, I'm in here on a probation violation. Me and my homeboy...I mean, a dude I used to mess with, sold a twenty-dollar rock to an undercover. I didn't make the sale, but the undercover saw me give it to him. They gave me two years probation for my first offense," Ray explained, without getting into the situation that placed him in the wheelchair.

"So what happened right there?" José asked, pointing at the wheelchair. "Some 'hood stuff gone bad?"

Ray didn't answer in an attempt to brush off the conversation.

José smiled. "Yeah," he said, shaking his head. "A lot can go wrong messin' around in the 'hood."

Chapter Thirteen

When the week finally started, Ray was hit with the destiny that he was trying to dodge: he was assigned to report to school. At first he was a little upset, but after figuring that there was no way around it, he did his best to be optimistic. *Besides,* he thought, *after what I've been spared from, goin' to school is a piece of cake.* So, when the time came to show up for classes, he did just that and gave it all of his attention. He figured since he had to go to school, he might as well get something out of it. A GED! *Momma Wilson will be so proud,* he thought.

Every other day he was required to see the physician, Doctor Brooks. On one occasion, he received some really good news. Doctor Brooks said the swelling had gone completely down around the bullet in Ray's back and he informed Ray that he would likely be out of his wheelchair in eight to twelve weeks. That gave Ray something to look forward to.

During therapy, and in the following weeks, Dr. Brooks had Ray do various stretches while he was in the chair to see how he was coming along. Seeing Ray's progress, the doctor informed him that in a few weeks he hoped Ray would be standing and doing stretches on his own.

"I don't want to rush anything," the doctor said. "I want you to take it easy and let this stuff come naturally for you. We don't want you to reinjure yourself."

Ray smiled. "That's cool, Doc," he agreed. He knew that he needed to get better, not worse.

When Trena's letter finally came, smelling like perfume, Ray was puppy-dog happy, though he tried to conceal his excitement from the rest of the guys around him. He refused to show any signs of weakness. Especially in an environment where most people were looking for someone to prey on. Trena expressed how she missed him and how he wasn't missing anything out on the streets. She spoke about a few dudes from his neighborhood who had been arrested, and how the police kept running up on people who hung out on the corners in an attempt to crack down on them selling drugs. She also mentioned how the police were still investigating Big Mack's and Sheila's murders.

That's why it's so hot on the Westside with police, she wrote. *If you're gangbangin', hangin' out in the streets sellin' dope, they're comin' at you. Ray, I'm scared and I wish you'd change before you come home because those streets don't have mercy for anyone. I know I haven't been up there yet to see you, but as soon as my dad lets me get away, I'll be up there, okay? He's been real protective lately, but the other night it surprised me when he came into my room and asked if you were all right. I told him you were, but it kind of shocked, scared, and surprised me all at the same time.*

Ray knew that Trena was her father's oldest child, and he had a right to be concerned about her well-being. Her father was a very good man in their community and everybody respected him. Ray understood why he had been so protective of her.

Ray continued to read Trena's letter in a low mumble.

Ray, I really like you, but I need you to try...just try....to be different. You're not a bad person. In fact, I see a lot in you, but you're caught up like everybody else. You're caught up in the streets! I can't be with somebody like that. I need you to try hard to change how you live so it won't be so hard for me when you come home. I love you, Trena.

Ray's mind jumped through hoops and shot fireworks. *She loves me*, he thought. The six-page letter moved and motivated him in more ways than one. He knew what he had to do. He knew that he had been harboring thoughts about what he wanted to do to C-Dog, while still reflecting on his life and everything that had been going on. He even became more conscious of the people around him, and how titles like "homeboy" could be more harmful than helpful if you were someone who bought into it. He thought about 1-Punch, Poochie, Joe-Joe, and Buff. Since he'd arrived at Nelles, he'd been referred to as "homeboy" by basically all four of them. He saw how, before he had gotten shot, all a person had to do was tell him that they were from the same block, neighborhood, city, or a city affiliate and he automatically welcomed them with open arms. *Not anymore*, he thought.

This made him look at everyone through different eyes. He vowed that everyone had to prove themselves before he would welcome them in. He immediately began to consider those around him. *Poochie is cool and unselfish*, he thought. *Joe-Joe is exactly the same laid back person that he has always been, and Buff is really mature and honest. And 1-Punch...* Ray contemplated and then shook his head.

Next, he noticed how everybody at Nelles was basically into gangs; or if they weren't into gangs, they were molded with that "gangsta" mentality. It didn't matter what time of day it was, he would see and hear Blacks, Mexicans, Whites, etc., holding conversations about doing drugs, selling drugs, having guns, shooting guns, shooting people, stealing cars, robbing stores and on and on, as if these things weren't the things that had gotten them all locked up. *They think this is all cool*, Ray thought. *Ain't nothin' cool about bein' in jail!*

Lastly, he watched as everyone twisted their faces and gritted their teeth at each other, like beefing would help them get home faster. He didn't understand this mentality, especially when more than ninety percent of them didn't even know each other.

When Ray went to the visiting room, it was packed. He could tell that a lot of the guys had family who loved them. When they went to visit, they had their standard blue shirts tucked into their state-issued blue jeans. He saw the mother of one of the boys smack him on top of his head when he walked out and forgot to leave his "gangsta stroll" in the unit.

That was one of the things Big Mack had taught him: It doesn't pay to bang. They were always trying to make money and Ray knew there was more than one way to get paid. If he had to, he'd get a good job. Anything but going back to jail.

* * *

Ray had written Trena back, reassuring her that he knew what he had to do. He told her he was in school and working on his GED. After he sent the letter off, it didn't take long for her to respond. She encouraged him to keep up the good work and told him she was trying her best to come see him soon.

Ray stayed to himself more than normal. He found time to have various discussions with José, while still respecting his space. 1-Punch must've caught a vibe, because he stayed far away. He slid through every now and then, usually after he came back from working out. But mostly it was Ray and José. They were ignorant of the fact that everyone was staring at them because they were so deeply engrossed in their discussions. They started talking in the afternoons when they came in from school and work, took a break for dinner, then continued until the lights went out at ten o'clock.

Ray expressed to his newfound friend how he felt about life and how getting shot was beginning to change his whole outlook on it. One night as Ray sat on his bunk and José sat in Ray's wheelchair, Ray explained in a hushed tone everything that had happened to him. José's mouth hung wide open as Ray expressed how his friend had shot him. Ray paused, teary eyed, and looked around the dimly lit unit at most of the other wards, who were nicely tucked in their beds, asleep. The unit officer was missing from his station, and other wards sat around each other's bunks and conversed in a whisper. Ray turned his attention back to José, in hopes that his eyes were dry. He continued to explain how his big brother — his mentor and idol — had gotten blown away by his best friend, and how this same person killed a girl who had helped set up the robbery. Ray told him this because something in his heart told him that José was genuine; that he was sincere.

José was speechless as he sat staring at Ray.

"Man," Ray continued, choked up with bruised emotions. "It hurt me to see someone I trusted enough to get close to me turn on me like that." He paused again and allowed his eyes to roam the housing unit. He cleared his throat. "And to think I used to call him homeboy," he added, shaking his head.

When José heard Ray's story, he opened up himself. "You know, I grew up in a mostly Hispanic community with seven brothers and two sisters," he began, looking around to see if the unit officer had made it back to his station. "My mother and father have been together for almost thirty-five years now. But my father and brothers were part of the East Side Rivas. My father was a big-time factor in our 'hood, and all of my brothers followed in his footsteps."

Ray shrugged. "So, where they at now? I mean…"

José looked away. He exhaled slowly. "All of them are in the penitentiary. My dad and brothers, all of them have life sentences but one, Mario. He has fifty years. I'm the last man in my family and now I'm locked up, too. Only my sisters are left to look after my mother, and at times I feel like I let them down."

"Dang, man," Ray interjected in a sympathetic tone. "So, what are you in here for now?"

José looked at Ray with glossy eyes. He rubbed his palms together and steepled his fingers. He placed them to his lips and said, "One night, me and my homeboys were pulled over with all kinds of guns in the car. It's a trip, though, because we were gonna go shoot up some Black Vatos who sold drugs a few blocks from where my mom lives."

Ray hesitated in confusion. *Black dudes?* he thought. "Why were you gonna let them have it? I mean…what'd they do?"

José shook his head, and then dropped his eyes toward his shoes. "I don't know, to be honest. We were high and…"

Ray started to interject, but suddenly paused. The guy in the bed next to him squirmed, as if waking up. Ray looked at José. "And what?"

José shrugged his shoulders. "Well, see, in Riverside the Tiny Dukes and the Black gangs have been beefin' for a long time," he explained. "I've heard a million stories about why, but none of them make any sense to me now. It took for God to have me arrested for me to see that I was on the same road as my father and brothers. That, and when I was in Juvenile Hall my mom had a heart attack and was in the hospital for a long time. When she got better she came to see me with my sisters and they asked me to change before it broke my mother's heart and she died."

Ray's heart felt as though it had flipped inside out as he listened quietly to José's story. Just the thought of him doing something else that would break Momma Wilson's heart again, or causing her to die, made him tear up on the inside.

José looked at Ray with sadness etched on his face. "After that," he continued, "I got a letter from my dad. He's up in San Quentin and he tells me that he doesn't want me in the gang. At first I felt betrayed. I mean, this was my idol. He was my image of a real life gangster and he was tellin' me to get out! But then he went on to explain how God revealed to him that family, blood, was more important than a gang. How my mother and sisters needed me. At that moment everything came rushin' down on me so fast." José paused and stared at Ray. He bit his lip, then softly continued. "My life took a spin when my mom had a heart attack. I started to look at how everyone is locked up, my dad, my brothers, and now me. I looked at how none of my so-called homeboys had looked out for me and I really felt like a fool. My dad was right. I couldn't keep livin' like I was without receivin' the same results as they did — or worse. So that night I got down on my knees and prayed for the man upstairs to come into my life. I asked Him to help me be better, to change my ways."

Ray continued to listen as José unloaded a wealth of insight.

"Ray, I still ask myself every day what this beef between us and you guys is all about, because it started before I was born. I went to school and grew up around Blacks all my life, so I don't dislike you guys," he said with emphasis. "I asked my dad about it and he told me that the East Side Rivas and the Tiny Dukes teamed up with the 1200 Blocc Crips to take on enemies in other neighborhoods. Eleven of the homies got sentenced to a lot of time, so the Dukes and the 1200s fell out. Now it's supposed to be an ongoin' beef between the Blacks and the Mexicans. Somethin' that started in jail by the Mexican Mafia for us becomin' allies with Black gangs to attack our own people. They say La Eme offered the Tiny Dukes one way out. That's why we're beefin' with Blacks now."

Ray frowned. *We?* he thought. "Why do you say 'we' like you're still a part of it?"

José sounded defensive. "I didn't mean it like that," he replied, gesturing with his hands like a crossing guard.

"I was just speakin' about Mexicans from my neighborhood in general. It's been around a long time. You know, my grandfather had 'East Side Riva' tattooed inside of the curve of his thumb and index finger, just like my dad."

Ray shook his head with a surprised look on his face. He remembered a story that Big Mack had told him about a friend getting killed in prison behind a beef between the Blacks and Mexicans. *But that was personal,* Ray thought. "Is that really a true story?"

"Like I said, I really don't know, because all of this happened before I was born," José said, emphasizing his point.

"Why haven't you asked one of your homeboys in here?"

José shrugged. "I did, but they just always say somethin' like 'it goes way back.' No one knows the truth, except the ones who were there, I guess."

Ray thought about how different his life was compared to José's, but how they still shared a lot of things in common. "José," Ray said hesitantly, "how do you feel about us now?"

José smiled. "Man, there's no difference between any of us, whether Black, Mexican, White or whatever. I can't honestly say that I love God and not love my neighbor."

Chapter Fourteen

"Ray, wait up!"

Ray was coasting his wheelchair down the sidewalk toward the unit when he saw Joe-Joe running toward him.

"What's up?" he responded.

Joe-Joe caught up to him and asked, "Where you comin' from?"

"Doctor Brooks called for me just before class let out. He wanted to see how I was comin' along."

Joe-Joe nodded with a gloomy look in his eyes. "What did he say?" he asked, walking beside Ray with his head hung low.

Ray looked at him and paused. "He just be havin' me do some stretches and stuff. He puttin' that cold listenin' thing on my back and chest, and havin' me move around and stuff. He don't say too much."

"Oh yeah?" Joe-Joe mumbled.

"Yeah, he told me I'm gettin' well fast, too. Today I stood up," Ray said, looking at his friend.

This brought a smile to Joe-Joe's face. "Is that right? How did it feel?"

Ray smiled. "Cool. My legs were a little wobbly, but I'm not as bad as I thought. The doctor said the same thing, but he told me not to get too cocky. He wants me to keep chillin' in this chair for a while."

They made it to the door that led into the housing unit, and Joe-Joe just stood there staring at his shoes. Ray looked up at him standing there, still with the gloomy look on his face.

"What's up man? Somethin' on your mind?"

Joe-Joe dropped his head a little more and shrugged his shoulders. "Naw, you know. They let me off school and work early because I didn't feel good."

Ray turned in his wheelchair to face him. With a

concerned look in his eyes, he asked, "What's wrong?"

Joe-Joe shrugged again. "Nothin'...I don't know. I got a letter yesterday and it kind of got to me."

Ray saw plainly that his friend was troubled, and made a suggestion that they should go inside to continue their conversation. As soon as they made it to the housing unit, they noticed that there was barely anyone there. This, they both knew, was due to the fact that there was still twenty minutes before work and school were released.

As they went over to Ray's bunk, Joe-Joe sat down and opened up to him. "Man," he began, "you know after you and Big Mack got shot at my cousin's house, my brothers been lookin' for C-Dog."

Ray was shocked. He didn't understand how Joe-Joe knew who shot them. "What makes you think C-Dog did it?"

Joe-Joe twisted his lips up. "Look dawg, I ain't a snitch I..."

"I didn't say you were."

"So, there ain't no need in actin' like that. Plus ol' boy's been out there runnin' his mouth about it. Terri's mad and both my brothers want to smoke him because she could've been in the house, too. The whole 'hood's lookin' for the dude. What he did was scandalous and people wanna teach him a lesson."

Joe-Joe continued to inform Ray about what was going on in his mind about the situation, and how he felt worried for his bothers' lives. He really didn't want anything to happen to them. "I just don't want them to get hurt, Ray. I apologize. I know we supposed to ride for each other, but..."

Ray interjected as his demeanor changed. "Man," he began with a pause. He studied Joe-Joe before he spoke. "I understand. And all this 'ride for each other' stuff, I don't want nobody to do anything to ol' boy. He's gotta answer to me for what he did to me and Big Mack," Ray said, getting frustrated just thinking about C-Dog.

Joe-Joe had never heard Ray talk like that before, but he was glad he understood how he felt about his brothers.

"Man, just be cool," Ray continued. "Your family is gonna be straight. Don't trip."

Joe-Joe smiled and nodded his head as if saying thanks. As he began to walk away, everyone was getting off work and school, and soon count time came around. Ray hollered at Poochie after count cleared to see how he was doing. Seeing that everything was all right with him, he went back to his bunk only to be stopped by José.

"What's up, L'il Ray?"

Ray nodded. "Nothin' much. What you got goin' on?"

José smiled. "I'm on my way to Bible study. Why, you wanna go?"

Ray threw his hands up in the air as if someone had just screamed "freeze!" "Naw, I'm cool," he expressed.

José nodded. "I understand. Aye, if you have time I want you to read somethin' in the Bible that we're talkin' about tonight at service. It's a story about David and Goliath. It's in 1st Samuel Chapter 17. Read it all and I'll holler at you later."

"All right, if I get a chance, I'll read it."

"Just in case you get a chance," José said with a giggle, "you may need to get another Bible, because that's in the Old Testament. I got an extra one if you need it."

Ray laughed. "Yeah, all right." He knew his plans didn't include reading the Bible, and he could tell José sensed it.

José went to his bunk and retrieved a leather-bound Bible. "Here you go, just in case you don't feel like gettin' up," he said, still smiling. "You know, with injuries and medication and all."

That tickled Ray, because he knew for sure José

knew his intentions. "Thanks," he said, accepting the Bible. "I'll holla." *David and Goliath sounds familiar*, Ray thought. *I hope it's a good story!*

* * *

Poochie mixed up some type of concoction out of soup and chili, wrapped it in burrito shells, and passed them out to Ray and Joe-Joe with a smile on his face, like he was proud of himself.

"What ya'll lookin' at?" he asked, staring at the expressions on their faces.

Ray and Joe-Joe didn't hide the fact that the concoction looked suspicious. They both twisted up their faces when they looked at it.

"Dawg," Joe-Joe said, rubbing his stomach. "I know I'm fat, but…but I'm not gonna let you feed me anything that looks like that!"

"Yeah," Ray said, laughing with Joe-Joe. "I thought you said if we didn't go to dinner you were gonna fix a gourmet meal?"

Poochie looked a little discouraged. "Just taste one, man!" Poochie shoved a burrito in Ray's direction.

Ray hesitated, then laughed. He took the goulash-filled burrito and smiled. Not wanting to disappoint Poochie, who seemed to have put a lot of work into it, he tasted it.

"What it taste like? What it taste like?" Joe-Joe kept asking.

Poochie sighed. "Give him a chance to taste it, hungry hippo!"

"Shut up, Poochie!"

Ray chomped down the first bite and instantly took another. *Thumbs up! The burritos are like that!* he thought.

Poochie passed Joe-Joe one finally. "Yeah!" he exclaimed proudly. "Chef-Boy-R-Dee has done it again!"

Chapter Fifteen

Ray was called to Medical during class, so he rushed back to his housing unit to put his books away. While inside his unit, he noticed Counselor Steele sitting in his office with the door open. Ray sat his school supplies on his bed and wheeled himself to where Steele was sitting.

"Knock, knock."

Counselor Steele looked up. "Come in, Turner. What's on your mind?"

Ray shrugged his shoulders. "Uhhh, nothin' really."

Counselor Steele bobbed his head with a blank look on his face. "Well, what can I do for you?"

Ray paused for a second and then replied, "I don't know. I guess I was kinda wonderin' why you haven't seen me for my one-on-one. I mean, I've been here a few months now and we've only talked one time."

Steele sat looking at Ray in amazement. He finally cracked a smile. "I've never seen someone so adamant about one-on-one. I'm usually the only one who looks forward to them."

Ray sat with his hands clasped and resting in his lap. "Like I said, I don't know why I…I guess I wanted to make sure me and you were all right, and that I'm not on no bad terms with you."

Steele laughed. "Bad terms," he exaggerated, letting out another healthy chuckle. "Turner, believe it or not, I kinda like your style. And to be honest, I use one-on-ones to help those here who need help the most. Everyone here needs help, but some need it more than others."

"So we straight, then?"

He smiled. "We're straight. Now, just because I haven't called you, it doesn't mean I haven't been checkin' up on you. Your teacher, Mrs. Tucker, has told me you're doin' well. Your language is fairly good, but you need to brush up on your math. She informed me that when you do, she wanted to test you for the pre-GED."

Ray seemed to glow with appreciation when Steele said this.

"Doctor Brooks told me that you've been makin' all your appointments and schedules and you're comin' along great, Turner," Steele paused, sliding himself closer to his desk as if he wanted to be heard loud and clear. "I've been watchin' you and you don't even know it. I've seen how you interact with others in the unit. José Mendez, he's a good kid. I've watched four of his brothers come through here. He's different. You're keepin' good company. Plus, I'll never forget what you told Mrs. Wilson on the phone. About how you made a promise to God and how you wanted to change."

Ray put his hand under his chin and listened to the counselor.

"Turner," Steele continued, "just keep doin' what you're doin'. I'm proud of you."

Ray smiled and nodded. "Hey, thanks Steele," he said, feeling encouraged. "I gotta go holla at Dr. Brooks now."

*   *   *

Things seemed to be going according to Ray's plans. First, the doctor had been making him appointments for rehabilitation and therapy every day. A nurse had been assisting him in various exercises that called for him to get out of his wheelchair. Ray was now taking steps that began at a slow pace, and ended up at a pace a notch above where he started. He was standing in place and stretching to the left, right, up and as far as he could toward his toes. He even started using the rowing machine during therapy. The sessions were held almost every day and they left Ray sweaty, tired, and very sore. But it was worth it because he knew he was making progress.

Next was his schooling. Ever since Counselor Steele mentioned his teacher's idea to let him take the pre-GED, Ray had been studying extra hard. Even when he was not in school, he spent his extra time polishing up on all areas of his math. José had just gotten his GED the year before, so he began tutoring Ray whenever he needed him to. José helped to make his math easier by showing him how to use his knowledge about drug weights, percentages, and calculations in the same way he did math problems on paper. It worked out great.

* * *

"Hey baby, you look good."

Although Trena had yet to make it to see him, Momma Wilson didn't miss a beat. Every other week she came like clockwork to visit. This week was no different.

"Thanks, Momma," Ray replied. "What you been doin'?"

"To be honest, ever since that stuff happened to you and Macarthur, a lot of the church members and I been going out into different communities, talking to young people about gangs and violence related to drugs."

"You have?" Ray asked curiously. "Why would you do that?"

"Because we're trying to help save someone else's kids. I don't want anyone to go through what I'm going through because of you and Macarthur. Did you know that the city of San Bernardino has over three thousand gang members who sell drugs and do various violent drug-related crimes?"

Ray was quiet, but then he humbly asked, "Over three thousand, Momma?"

"Yeah, baby. They have gangs called California Gardens, Delmann Heights Bloods, IE Black Rag Mafie,

Five Time Hometown Crips, and not to mention the Magnolia Street Blood gang where we live. But the largest is the Verdugo Flats. I've learned all of this since you guys was shot."

While Ray sat and listened as Momma Wilson talked, a sharp pain ripped through his stomach when he thought about the hurt he'd caused her.

* * *

Trena's letters flowed through the mailbox like government checks. They always came on time! She explained how she and her father had had a long talk about Ray one night. Her dad had read a letter Ray wrote to her and came to her room. Trena said she was disappointed that her father had invaded her privacy, but when she gave him a chance to explain, she understood.

He just loves me, she went on to write. *And he is scared I'll make a bad decision. But he said he read your letter and saw how you spoke of your accomplishments in school and how you felt about the streets, and he told me that he believed in you. He told me that he always liked Big Mack and that he knew Mack's dad. He knows that you're all that Mrs. Wilson has left and he told me to tell you to make her proud and keep up the good work.*

That particular letter really motivated Ray in a big way. He wrote back that when he first got to Nelles he didn't want her lying to her dad so she could come to see him. He wanted her to respect her dad, because he had plans on getting her dad to like him. Now it looked like it was all panning out.

The final thing that was coming around for Ray was the growth of his understanding of the Bible. Spending time with José had really begun to pay off. The two of them would talk and, to Ray, it seemed that José would open up a side of Ray's thinking that he had never seen before. He knew that José's faith in God was what helped him to see life in such a positive way. This intrigued Ray and he told José how he felt. Ray expressed how he felt about his obligations to homeboys and the 'hood, and José would share some of the same views.

"Family is more important than a gang," José would always say, quoting some of the language his father wrote in letters.

Ray even went on to ask José his opinion on all the tension between the Blacks and the Mexicans. By this time both of them had noticed how individuals, and sometimes groups, would watch them talking to each other, but neither one of them cared. José went on to tell him how he thought it was all nonsense, something that was designed to keep his people and Ray's people from prospering.

"These guys are young, Ray," José began. "We all are. And to go straight from the cradle to the grave, livin' a life filled with hatred and violence, is a life wasted on foolishness. They don't know it yet, but there's no way to find peace or happiness livin' like that."

During this conversation José confided in Ray that he only had a couple of months left at Nelles. His time was winding down and he was going to be back on the streets again, able to help his mother and sisters.

"My oldest sister, Amelia, is nineteen now," he told Ray. "She has a boyfriend named Hector whose uncle has a business buildin' houses. Amelia told me he said when I get out I got a job waitin' for me makin' ten dollars an hour. You can't beat that at seventeen years old!"

Ray smiled, nodding his head. "Naw, that's not bad!"

"I know, man. That's why you have to try to keep your head in the right places. I've seen a lot of my homeboys, my so-called friends, come and go, talkin' about doin' good when they get out. But right after they make it home they sent us pictures of them doin' the same old things."

Ray shook his head and leaned backwards. He had a serious look on his face. "Man, I'm straight, José."

José stared at Ray with a blank look in his eyes. "I hope so, because we heard about a lot of them gettin' shot and killed. But sometimes if they're lucky, they just end up back in jail. It's like they lose their way and forget what they've been through."

Ray's facial expression turned serious. "Man, this is on everything, José," he began, shaking his head and looking around the building. "I'll never forget this experience!"

Chapter Sixteen

Ray was nervous. Poochie kept telling him to be cool, but he couldn't help it. Buff had told him that there was nothing to worry about, but it didn't feel that way. He was bubbling with anticipation and fear.

"Mail call!"

Ray knew it was on its way. His teacher told him to look for it. Now, waiting in the clustered group of young men, he held his breath in anticipation of his name being called.

"Turner," the officer yelled out.

"Here I go." Ray grabbed the paper and made his way over to his bunk. José, Joe-Joe, Poochie, and Buff all waited on him to tell them the news.

Ray looked up at José with sweat beads forming on his forehead. "José, open it for me." Ray handed the folded piece of paper, which was stapled at the top, to his tutor, who opened it immediately.

José looked it over thoroughly and then simply said, "It's 456. You passed. No *problema*!"

Ray's heart jumped. He knew he had to score at least a 450 on his pre-GED to pass, but a 456! Everyone was happy for him because they knew how hard he had worked for it.

"See," Joe-Joe told Poochie. "I told you he'd do it!" Then he turned to Ray and said, "Poochie's been in the class goin' on ten years. He's almost twenty with a beard and everything. The teacher told him that he'd need another ten years to pass the pre-GED!" he exclaimed with a outburst of laughter.

Everyone started laughing at Poochie, who took it on the chin. "That's all right," he laughed. "I'm only bad in math. Probably just as bad as you are in spellin'!"

The expression on Joe-Joe's face was dumbfounded.

"Spellin'? I'm not bad in spellin'!"

Poochie smiled. "Oh, is that right?"

"Yeah, my spellin' is superb!"

"Well, spell 'diet' then, fat boy!"

When Poochie said this everybody laughed even harder. He'd gotten Joe-Joe back on that one.

* * *

Ray smiled, showing all thirty-two teeth. Momma Wilson had come for a visit, like she always did, but this time she brought along a friend.

"Momma, I really passed my pre-GED," Ray emphasized, giving Momma Wilson a hug.

"You passed!" she said with a look of surprise. "You know I'm proud of you."

"Me, too," Trena said, trying to conceal her joy at seeing Ray for the first time since he'd been at Nelles. "Ray, we are so proud of you," Trena continued. "I can't wait to tell my dad."

"Yeah," Ray responded with an infinite smile. "Man, you look different, like...like if you're...I don't know..."

Trena blushed. "Like what?" she questioned softly.

Ray shrugged. "I don't know, like you're more grown up or somethin'," he said, trying to explain. "I mean, your eyes are different, or, like, serious."

Momma Wilson interjected. "It's probably because you haven't seen her in a few months. I've seen that look before."

Ray smiled. "What look, Momma?"

Momma Wilson shook her head. "Boy, that puppy dog look when someone's in love," she added with a giggle.

"Momma!"

Trena blushed uncontrollably. "Mrs. Wilson!"

Momma Wilson waved them off with a hand

gesture. "I'm just playing with you kids."

They looked at each other until their eyes drifted toward the ground.

"And what in God's name made you cut your hair?" Momma Wilson asked.

Ray knew that one was coming. Ever since he could remember, he'd had long hair. Momma Wilson had never seen him any other way. No one had, for that matter. A few days prior to his visit, he asked Poochie to cut his hair into a bald fade, which left his head bald on the sides, and tapered into a low cut on the top, since Poochie occasionally cut hair in various styles. To Ray, it felt strange not to have hair on his head, but it also felt right, too.

"I don't know, Momma," he answered sheepishly. "I just wanted a new look. Somethin' that didn't make me look like a thug."

Trena smiled at his answer. "Ray, you look cute like that."

Ray tried to cover his smile with his hand, but his blush revealed it.

"You're right, Trena. He does look like a handsome young man." As Momma Wilson said this, Ray's attention was drawn to a woman who seemed to be fussing. When he looked, he noticed that 1-Punch was visiting with someone Ray assumed to be his mother. She was dressed in a nurse's uniform. To Ray she looked to be mad.

"Wesley, money don't grow on trees," she yelled at him. "I can't keep sendin' you money every time you get ready to ask for it!"

"I know, Momma," 1-Punch said in a voice that sounded like a four-year-old child's.

"And sit up straight, you're slouchin'! You still in school?"

1-Punch nodded. "Yeah."

"Yeah? Boy, who you talkin' to?" she raised her

hand, gesturing toward her son.

1-Punch flinched. "I'm sorry, Momma."

"What did I teach you, Wes?"

"To say 'yes, ma'am,'" he interjected.

1-Punch's mother pointed her finger at him. "That's right, boy. Don't ever forget I'm yo' Momma, not one of those wannabe gangstas you hang out with. That's ya'lls problem now, wannabe gangstas. I grew up with real gangstas and they didn't act like ya'll stupid butts."

Ray listened as she went completely off. He couldn't believe how well mannered 1-Punch was compared to when he was in the dorm. But Ray also knew she was right, and 1-Punch was getting his issue with her.

For the remainder of the afternoon Ray enjoyed the visit he had dreamed about for so many nights. He finally had both of the women he cared about the most in the same room. Trena asked him dozens of questions about his time at Nelles. Was it rough? Did people bother him? He simply told her that he was fine and doing well. Trena then went on to explain how her father had agreed to let her visit him, but she had to be home by one o'clock. He had called Momma Wilson to make sure that she was going to be present and, of course, she was.

"He just wanted to make sure you guys won't be up here smoochin' and houchin'," Momma Wilson said with a laugh.

Ray looked confused. "Momma, what's smoochin' and houchin'?" he asked inquisitively.

"Boy, you know what it is!" Momma Wilson smiled, rolling her eyes. "But Trena's dad asked me to make sure nothing like that goes on, so if you don't know, you won't be finding out today."

Trena and Ray laughed at Momma Wilson's play of humor.

"Ray," Trena said on a more serious note. "I'm really proud of you. I want you to keep up the good work.

Not for us," she said, looking at Momma Wilson. "But, do it because you believe you can do it. Do it for yourself, okay?"

Ray nodded. "I got you."

*　　*　　*

"How was your visit?" José asked as Ray came through the door.

Ray smiled. "Wonderful."

"That's good to hear, man."

Just when Ray was telling José about how 1-Punch's mother showed out on him, he noticed Counselor Steele come out of his office.

"Turner!" he called out. "Let me see you in my office."

It was another off day for Steele, but as usual he came to work to maintain the stability of the environment. That, plus he did his best to be there for the guys under his supervision.

"What's up, Steele?"

"Close the door," Steele instructed.

Ray did as he was told and gave Counselor Steele his undivided attention.

"Turner, I talked to your probation officer, Tom Upshaw, a few days ago. He also called me back this mornin'."

Oh nooo… Ray thought.

"He wanted a report on your progress, which I sent to him on Wednesday. He was curious to know about your status for the last thirty days. Now, normally he just calls and asks about different people, so I don't know what's up this time. This mornin' I talked to him and he was curious to know the scores you made on your pre-GED. So, I pulled your files and faxed him a copy of the results. He seemed to be impressed."

Ray was glad to hear that everything seemed to be cool, so he just continued to listen.

"He went on to tell me that he planned on comin' to visit you soon, so I want you to keep up the good work, all right?"

Ray nodded his head. "All right."

"That'll be all, you can go now."

Ray wheeled himself out of Steele's office just as a young Mexican guy walked in and brushed up against him. He was thinking so much about his probation officer that he didn't pay any attention to the guy who bumped into the arm of his wheelchair without saying "excuse me."

Chapter Seventeen

"Chow time, chow time! If you're goin' to eat, let's go!"

The officer called for the evening meal just as Ray and José were engaged in a deep conversation.

"You goin'?" José asked Ray.

"Yeah, man, I'm starvin'!"

"Me too. Let's go," José said, grabbing the back of Ray's wheelchair in an attempt to push him into the crowd.

Ray looked at José. "I got this," he insisted.

José smiled. "What's wrong, you don't want your homeboys to see a Mexican pushin' you?"

Ray looked at him sideways. "Man, you know how I feel about what other people think. But for reals, I ain't trippin'. Be my guest."

Ray and José followed the other young men to the chow hall in a single-file line. They stood in line with the others waiting to get their meals. As they reached the serving line and retrieved their trays, they noticed that dinner was breaded veal patties, mashed potatoes, brown gravy, and peas. José handed Ray both their trays and headed straight for a table to sit down. They were part of the last group to eat, so they sat at the same table, right next to each other. Once they were seated, neither of them said a word to each other the whole time they were eating. As soon as they were finished, José dumped their trays. They left the hall the same way they came in, with José pushing Ray in his wheelchair. As soon as they made it back to their unit, they heard voices arguing from inside. Curious, they rushed in to see what was going on.

"Listen, holmes, this is our table. You and your homies over there need to keep to yourselves."

Ray and José watched as Javier stood with a group of his friends. They were confronting an aggressive looking

1-Punch, who was standing with some of the friends he had been hanging out with over the past few months.

Instinctively, Ray looked around and saw Poochie and Joe-Joe standing near their bunks, looking in the direction of the commotion while Buff stood with his arms folded in a far corner.

1-Punch bowed his back to push his chest out. "Ya'll don't own nothin' around here! That's ya'll problem now!"

Instantly the unit officers responded to the commotion. "Break it up! Break it up!" they hollered to the small group that had congregated. After seeing that the group didn't budge, and they were still standing, engaged in a stare down/standoff, the officers proceeded to plan B. "Get on your racks, now! Let's go! Now!"

José continued pushing Ray to his bunk.

"Man, we hit!" Ray said, looking up at José.

"Yup. We'll probably be on our bunks for the rest of the night."

*   *   *

The next morning Ray awoke and stretched before getting out of his bunk. He grabbed his toothbrush and toothpaste. As he was on his way to the bathroom, he overheard an ongoing conversation. He recognized one of the voices and stopped. By the sound of the broken accents, it seemed like the person was having an argument with another Mexican guy.

"So what you sayin', *esse*?" he asked.

"José, you know what I'm sayin'! Those Black dudes are our enemies. How are you kickin' it with them?" someone asked him.

"Yeah," another voice interjected. "You don't kick it with the homies like that. Not to mention we're still beefin' with those fools."

After hearing the voices again, Ray immediately recognized whose voice it was: Javier's. "José, holmes, you make the 'hood look bad. You need to stop messin' with that one Black Vato. The homeboys on the streets are gonna think somethin's funny with you."

Ray wished he hadn't pulled up on the conversation. He didn't want to hear José choose between him and his friends.

"So, is that all you have to say?" José asked. "If so, I want all of you to listen close because I don't want to repeat myself. Your beef ain't my beef! I'm my own man and I'll do whatever I want to. If any of you have a problem with that, we can handle it right now."

Ray shook his head. He was about to advance, but something told him to hold his peace.

"José, if it wasn't for your brothers and father..." Javier began, but was instantly cut off by José.

With frustration José screamed, "Brothers and father what? Didn't you hear what I said?" he barked at the top of his lungs. "I'm my own man and with me it's family before a gang, *esse*. I don't need to stand on my father's or brothers' reputations! You know me, *esse*!"

Ray continued to listen.

"We're not talkin' about family!" Javier continued. "We're talkin' about messin' with that Black fool!"

"No, you're the fool, Javier. Whosoever does the will of my Father in Heaven is my brother, so that's my family. So like I said, if you got a *problema* with that, we can handle it right now."

Ray sat and listened as no one responded to José's statement. And then, to his surprise, Javier and two other guys exited the bathroom. Javier saw Ray sitting to the side against the wall and gave him a cross look. José stormed out of the bathroom fast. He was so upset that he never looked in Ray's direction. He kept walking straight to his bunk, where he flopped down and opened his Bible.

For the rest of the morning and afternoon, Ray was in complete awe. He had never met anyone like José. He literally stood up for what he believed, and he did it with strength. Ray had met people who stood up for their neighborhoods and gangs, but never had he met anyone like José, who stood up *against* his gang for a friendship. Ray was contemplating these thoughts when he noticed 1-Punch standing with a few guys looking his way.

"Yo, Ray, what's up? Why you over here lookin' like you all lost?"

Ray shook his head. It was Buff. He had just come in from working out.

"Ahh, man, I'm just thinkin', that's all," Ray replied.

Buff wiped the sweat from his brow. "Yeah, I get like that too sometimes, you know?"

Ray nodded. "Yeah, I can feel you."

"What's the Doc sayin' about gettin' rid of that 'Lac?"

Ray smiled because he knew that Buff was talking about his wheelchair. "He told me I should be out of it in a couple more weeks. I feel like I'm ready now because I've been walkin' around exercisin' and everything."

"Yeah, when you do, I'mma help you put on a few pounds before you bounce."

When Buff said this, he did it with a smile. Ray looked at him and said, "Naw, homie, I'm cool. My girl likes me just like this."

Buff laughed at how Ray bowed his arms and flexed his chest. "Aye man, I was just try'nah help. 'Cause I'm tellin' you, if you add a little weight to what you're doin', it'll help you get your strength back fast."

Ray looked at Buff, bobbing his head and letting the air out of his chest. "That's what's up then. I might get at you on the low, you feel me?"

Buff nodded. "Holla at me, homie, I got you whenever you're ready. But, I gotta hit the showers now, so

I'll holla at'chu later."

That's a cool dude, Ray thought as Buff walked away. He liked how he carried himself, not to mention how he treated people, even though he was such a big guy. *Normally, a person with as many muscles as Buff would definitely be a bully*, Ray thought.

One day Joe-Joe told Ray that Buff had been in Juvenile Hall for almost five years. He had beaten up on his mother's boyfriend one night because he was slapping her around. Joe-Joe went on to tell Ray that Buff had jumped on the man and had brutally beaten him. He broke his jaw, his arm, and four ribs. The District Attorney prosecuted him because the arresting officer said he wouldn't stop beating the man after the police arrived. The police busted in the house and Buff was still slamming and busting the man up. This was a crazy story, Ray thought, because back then when all this was supposed to have occurred, Buff was only fourteen years old. Since Buff's arrest, his mother hadn't come to see him once.

Ray laughed to himself as he thought about the story Joe-Joe told him. He wondered how much of it was truth and how much of it was fiction.

Just as Ray slid into his wheelchair, he was approached by 1-Punch and the small group of guys he stood with.

"L'il Ray," he said sarcastically. "Let me get at you, gangsta."

Ray felt something was amiss. *What does 1-Punch want?* he thought. He leaned back in his chair, trying to keep his cool, anxious to see what 1-Punch wanted.

"What's up, dawg?" 1-Punch asked as he walked up to Ray. He stood with his legs slightly spread apart, and his head cocked to one side. He gave his best impersonation of a gangster.

I wish 1-Punch's mother could see him now, Ray thought. "You tell me, what's up?"

"Naw, homie, you tell me," 1-Punch told him with attitude. "You're the one around here carryin' it like you soft or somethin'."

Instantly Ray felt his blood begin to boil, but he managed to keep his cool. "What do you mean, soft? I'm not sure what you talkin' about, man."

By this time Joe-Joe and Poochie had started to make their way over toward the scene. Ray also saw a few Mexican guys looking on from afar. He saw José in his peripheral vision.

"I'm talkin' about how you 'round here actin' like a buster, readin' books and Bibles and stuff. You up in here like the Westside taught you that. The Westside breeds ri'dahs! Not soft suckas who mess with Mexicans!"

Ray's expression became cold. "So, this is what this is all about?" he exclaimed.

When 1-Punch made this remark, Ray noticed that the few Mexican guys who were sitting at the table slowly started to get up. Ray quickly glanced toward the officers' desk and noticed that the officer on duty was reading a newspaper. He slid one of his feet from the wheelchair footrests onto the floor. He looked up at 1-Punch and said, "Check this out, playboy. I don't know what you think you see in me, but ain't nothin' soft over here. You're hollerin' Westside, and you ain't done nothin' but get in a few recess fights in school." Ray lifted his shirt and displayed the long slash that went from the center of his chest to his stomach. "I took mine for the 'hood I represented. I ain't take nobody down when they tried to kill me." Ray's nostrils flared. "You're still walkin' around without the slightest scar, like you just came out of your momma's womb!"

He could tell 1-Punch was upset, but he continued.

"The difference between you and me is I'm a vet at seventeen. You're not! I call my own shots. You don't. I know when it's time to lay down, while you're gonna make somebody lay you down!"

Just then 1-Punch took a step forward with his fist balled so tight you could see the white on his knuckles. "You crippled punk! I'll..."

Ray was too quick. In one swift motion he stood up and threw a straight-handed jab that hit 1-Punch square in the jaw. The blow was so vicious that the impact signaled the officer's attention. He dropped his newspaper as he witnessed 1-Punch beginning his descent to the floor.

"Break it up! You hear me? Break it up!" the officer yelled, running toward the gathering.

By the time the officer made it over to the scene, Ray was sitting back in his wheelchair with 1-Punch knocked out cold at his feet. But it was too late. The officer had seen Ray standing. He knew Ray had done it. There was still a small group of people standing around and Poochie and Joe-Joe were among them.

"Turner!" the officer yelled at Ray. "Let's go!"

* * *

It was dark as Ray sat in his wheelchair, staring at the small window. He shook his head, allowing his eyes to refocus as the smell of mold seeped into his nostrils. He gazed around the eight-by-ten cell that had a dingy, stainless steel sink and toilet. The green plastic mattress covering had cracks in it, and it sat on top of a steel bunk without any bedding. His heart was heavy. He dropped his head in disbelief. He didn't even care about his surroundings. He was too consumed with his thoughts...thoughts that were hyperactive, running a hundred miles per hour through his head.

What the... He had it comin'! Man, I messed up... 1-Punch was knocked out! He ain't got no scrap game... Momma Wilson's gonna be upset... Upshaw's comin' up here, man... Trena! Her dad! Why couldn't I let it go? I put that work in... Man that was stupid... How did I let that sucka get me to lose my cool? I'm sorry, Big Mack! I'm sorry...God!

Hours later, Ray still sat in his wheelchair, feeling like he had made the stupidest mistake of his life. In his mind he wrestled back and forth between thoughts about the first time Big Mack took him to McDonald's, to the day Mack was murdered. The truth was, he really wanted to go home, but he also wanted to teach 1-Punch a lesson. It wasn't worth it. He knew that what he did to 1-Punch wasn't worth the cost of not going home. It wasn't worth the cost of him messing up his life because of what someone thought about him.

Soon his mind drifted to images of him and Big Mack riding in Mack's low-ride Impala. Ray began to cry. His big brother, mentor and idol...was dead. He thought about the streets that took him. He thought about C-Dog. And then he thought about the promise he made to God — the same promise he knew he had broken. Ray sat in sorrow with his head hung low. He screamed out loud, clenching his fists. "Lord, I can't keep livin' like this!"

Right then he felt weak and alone. Images of José came into his mind. The thought that they both were the only ones left to take care of their families... *You're right, José,* he thought. *Family before anything, especially a gang!*

Ray exhaled heavily. "God, man, I don't wanna be this way anymore. I don't wanna act like this. I'm sorry. I'm sorry..."

The tears began to stream down his face. Ray didn't like the fact that he had broken a promise. He always kept his word.

"Forgive me, Lord," Ray continued, lowering his voice to a soft, quivering whisper. "Forgive me for messin' up. I didn't mean to break my promise. I didn't mean to do it. I just need help stayin' strong. Please forgive me!"

As Ray spoke these words, everything around him

disappeared. Soon he drifted off to sleep.

Chapter Eighteen

Ray didn't know how long he had been asleep, but he figured it was basically all night long. The sound of keys jingling and muffled voices woke him. Someone was coming. He heard a key being inserted into the cell's door lock and "clack," it opened up.

"Turner! Turner, you…what the…"

It was Counselor Steele.

"Ya'll didn't give him any sheets or covers?" he asked a correctional officer angrily.

"Hey Steele, I wasn't here last night," was all the officer had a chance to say.

Ray looked up and saw Counselor Steele shake his head at the officer. "All right, let me talk to him."

The officer left. Steele's cocky frame loomed in the doorway. Ray knew he was in for it, but by this point, he had lost hope. He felt like he'd really tried to change his ways, but because he broke his promise to God it was all over. He might as well change back to his old self.

"Turner, what happened?"

Ray slid his legs to the floor and shook off the discomfort he felt because of the lonely plastic mat he had slept on. He didn't know what to say. "I slipped, Steele," Ray said, shrugging his shoulders. "1-Punch came at me with some crazy stuff and I…"

Counselor Steele cut him off. "Hold up! Hold up! You let a stupid fool like Wesley Johnson get in your way?"

"But…"

Steele shook his head. "No buts! I'm not gonna let you use Johnson as your excuse. Not this time, son. You got in your own way, that's what happened!"

Ray dropped his head. When he lifted it, he had a mean look in his eyes. But Steele continued.

"You're gonna have to make a choice and stick to it, Turner. All that tough guy, gangsta garbage ain't gonna get you nowhere in life. Ain't no love in those streets! It's 'homeboy' today and 'stab you in the back' the next."

That was it. Ray couldn't take any more. "How are you gonna tell me somethin'?" he asked, projecting anger through the tone in his voice. "How would you know? It ain't like you think it is on the streets, because you probably grew up in Beverly Hills somewhere."

Counselor Steele laughed and shook his head while Ray continued.

"It's hard! It's tough! And people will try you like a pair of jeans. When they do, you gotta stand up for yours. So that's what I did! But you'll never understand that because you ain't ever been to the 'hood!"

Counselor Steele stood listening to Ray, no expression on his face. Then, all of a sudden, he shook his head and walked out. Steele called the officer to lock the door behind him. A part of Ray wondered where Steele went and the other part didn't care. One thing he knew for certain was that Counselor Steele left him sitting exactly where he was.

As he sat attempting to gather his thoughts, not even ten minutes had passed before he heard the jingle of keys again. The door unlocked once again, and when it did, Ray looked up and saw Counselor Steele standing there with a small book in his hand.

"Here," Steele said, throwing the book to Ray. "Look at these."

Steele walked into the cell and took a seat on the bed where Ray had slept the night before. Ray opened the book and came face-to-face with a small collection of pictures. It was a miniature photo album. Ray's eyes searched over the photos, taking in every detail, inch by inch. Counselor Steele was in each picture, dressed in prison blues. He was younger and built like the Incredible

Hulk.

"I did fifteen years in the system," he began to explain. "Chino, Corcoran, Quentin, Tracy, when it was called gladiator school. You name it, I've been there."

Ray couldn't believe what he was seeing or hearing.

Steele jammed his index finger into the crease of his chest. "I grew up in South Central L.A. in a neighborhood called the Main Street Mafia Crips. I was known and I was feared. I went to the pen at eighteen years old for second degree murder."

Steele paused to let the words sink in. Ray was still looking at the photos in front of him.

"I was in Quentin when I decided to change, and give my life to the Lord. At first my homeboys acted funny about it because they weren't used to change. But I wasn't trippin' on that. When they saw me constantly strivin' to better myself, and they saw that I was serious, they stopped actin' funny toward me. See, your true friends, your real homeboys, will support you no matter what."

Ray found himself nodding his head in agreement. He began to understand Steele more.

"Believe it or not, it was a man named Chico Mendez who witnessed to me in Quentin. Do you know who that is?"

Ray shook his head. He didn't make the connection with the name. "Naw, who is it?"

Steele looked at him and smiled. "That's José's dad."

"José's dad!"

"Yeah. See, Turner, when I read your file and saw what you've been through, I saw a young man whose life was spared. I took an oath after I changed my life that when I got out of prison, I would help as many at-risk youths as I could, and work in gang prevention. I've been a counselor for ten years or so now. Every time I see a young kid in here, my heart goes out to him. But it's one out of maybe every twenty that really wants to change. That's what I saw when I saw you. I saw in you the desire to change."

Ray nodded again.

"Turner," Steele continued, studying Ray. "When you first came here I asked you three specific questions. I'm still waitin' on two of the answers. See, I ask all of my boys these questions because each and every one of you gets a fresh start in life when you turn eighteen years old. Your criminal record will be sealed as if you've never been in trouble before. So, my remaining questions to you today are, what are you trying to accomplish? And what do you really want out of life?"

Ray hesitated. "I guess just to get my GED, and try to look out for Momma Wilson," he said, unsure of himself.

"That's all, Turner? The sky is the limit as to what you can accomplish and that's all you can see yourself accomplishing?"

Ray shrugged his shoulders. "I mean, get me a nice ride, but…"

Steele interjected with a look of disappointment etched on his face. "Turner," he began with a slight pause. "My way out of those streets started when I accepted Christ into my life. From there, I set a goal to become what I am today. But you, you can become anybody, anybody you want to become, even the President."

Ray looked at Steele attentively without saying a word.

"Look what happened in 2008 with Barack Obama becomin' our first African-American president. That has changed the landscape of the playin' field, because now you don't have any excuse to limit your dreams. See, everything in life has a price and that price is called sacrifice. Everyone from Dr. Martin Luther King to President Obama who has discovered the key to levelin' the playin' field of life has discovered it through education. They understood that it doesn't matter if you're Black, White, Mexican,

Asian, or Native American. There is only one way to balance the scales of equality, because physically we'll always have different traits. But mentally, through knowledge and intellect, you can balance the playin' field."

Ray looked confused. "But how do I go about doin' that?" he questioned curiously.

Steele smiled. "Turner, you begin by wantin' more than just you're GED," he answered softly. "You begin by wantin' to further your education, because the more info you have available to you that can be utilized in your life, the more options you have besides goin' back to those same old streets. If it worked for President Obama, it'll work for you, as well. He's no different than you are. He just made the right decisions at the right time. Besides, wouldn't you like to see that young girl you've been writin' become the first lady of the United States?"

Ray's eyes shone like Christmas lights. He had heard enough and closed the book. "Counselor Steele, I apologize for judgin' you. Man, sometimes people try to judge another person, when they could never imagine what it's like to walk in his shoes. Ol' boy 1-Punch was just stupid. He kept actin' like I was supposed to act all hard 'cause I got shot, like that's gangsta or somethin'. Then, when I didn't, he wanted to call me soft for try'nah get my GED and readin' the Bible. But I kept my cool for a minute. It wasn't until he accused me of bein' wrong for kickin' it with José when I got mad." Ray dropped his head again.

Steele shook his head, and spoke with disappointment in his voice. "Was it worth it, son? Was riskin' everything you've worked for over these past few months worth losin' it all, and stayin' here for the remainder of your violation…or longer?"

"Naw, man. It wasn't worth it," Ray answered, hunching his shoulders. "Ain't nothin' worth my freedom. I just messed up, man."

Counselor Steele listened to him and knew that his

heart was sincere. "José's father taught me one very important thing: we all make mistakes. But the most important part of makin' a mistake is how we recover from it. I came in here because as soon as I got to work, I had at least thirty kids at my door waitin' on me. Mexicans, Blacks, Whites, and I wanna say a couple of Asian boys. They all spoke up for you. They all want you out."

Ray didn't know what to say. He stuttered. "What do you mean, 'recover'?"

Steele paused. He placed his hand over his mouth and rested his chin in his palm. He looked Ray directly in his eyes. "Recover, meanin' you can land on your feet and get right back on track where you left off, doin' good. Or you can land on your butt and fall back into your old ways. You have a choice in determinin' how you want to recover from any situation in your life."

Ray sat despondent. "I feel you."

"Come on, man. I'm going to spring you loose, but you gotta promise me two things."

Ray looked hesitant. "What's that?"

"That you'll think the next time someone tries to get you off your square, and you'll work hard on your GED."

Ray thought for a moment and said, "I can do that. I promise."

Steele cracked a smile. "Well, all right. You're outta here."

As Steele turned to lead the way, Ray called out to him. "Yo' Steele."

Counselor Steele looked at him with his same smile. "I got'chu. What did I tell you? Just do as you promised and I got your back."

Ray felt relief. He wheeled his chair out of the small cell and into the hallway. Quickly he looked up and mumbled, "Good lookin' out, man."

Steele went into his office and Ray began wheeling himself toward his bunk. When he did, he noticed everyone around him staring. It seemed like smiles and nods were shot his direction, indicating everyone was glad he was back. He even caught a glimpse of Javier sitting at a card table. He looked at Ray and nodded in acknowledgement. His nod signified respect.

"Yo', L'il Ray. Aye Ray!"

Ray looked up and Joe-Joe, Poochie, Buff, and José were making their way over to him. Poochie stood behind him and pushed, while the other three walked beside him.

"Man, we went to bat for you this mornin'," Poochie told him proudly.

"Yeah, everybody did," Joe-Joe added.

"Yeah, man, even the Mexicans," José commented. "Javier and his boys personally talked to Counselor Steele about gettin' you out. They said 1-Punch isn't gonna come back. He was the main one startin' all of the stuff between everybody."

It figures, Ray thought as he looked back on it.

"Man, L'il Ray," Buff began. "You knocked 1-Punch clean out of his socks."

Ray gave off a humble smirk. "I know, but I wish I hadn't done it."

"But he had it comin'," Joe-Joe vouched.

"Yeah," José agreed. "He was around here pressin' his luck."

Ray took in what they all had just said, and then a thought came to mind. "Ma-a-a-n, ya'll wanna here somethin' crazy?"

They were all ears. "Yeah, what's that?" Poochie and Joe-Joe asked simultaneously.

"Did you know that Counselor Steele..." He decided not to finish what he was about to say. Something made him bite his tongue. He wanted to tell them about the pictures and how Steele was from South Central, but he thought about it and began to realize that Counselor Steele may not want everyone in his business.

"Counselor Steele what?" Buff asked anxiously.

Ray shook his head. "Never mind."

Real homeboys will support you, no matter what!

Chapter Nineteen

"Playboy, playboy, playboy, what's crack-a-lack'n?"

Ray shook his head. Officer Upshaw was something else.

"Come on up in this thang and pop slick wit'chu, boy."

Officer Upshaw had finally made it up to Nelles to see him. It was a brand new week and Ray was feeling great. Trena and Momma Wilson had both come to see him Saturday and Sunday. Both were looking happy and full of life. The only downside to the visit was when Trena gave him some surprising news. Someone had found C-Dog dead, shot two times in the head while sitting in his SUV. It happened at a gas station on California Street and Highland Avenue, a few days prior to them coming to see him. The news shocked Ray, but not as much as when Steele told him that Upshaw would be there the following day. All Ray hoped for was that his name wasn't caught up in the mix.

Now his probation officer sat in Counselor Steele's office behind the desk, looking just as crazy as Ray last remembered him. "How you been hangin'?" he asked Ray.

"Man, Upshaw, I've been makin' it."

Upshaw nodded toward the wheelchair. "What are they saying about the chair? You've been in that thing about three and a half months now, right?"

Ray knew this was all small talk, so he played along. "Dr. Brooks told me I should be out sometime this week."

"Ummm, that's good, that's good. Look..." Upshaw hesitated while he opened a manila folder that sat on the desk. Then he said, "I'm really impressed with the progress you've been making since you've been here. Counselor Steele said your conduct has been impeccable and you've been instrumental in bringing about peace between the

Blacks and the Mexicans up here. I heard they were at war at one point in time."

Instrumental? Ray thought. *I knocked out the main guy startin' all the trouble!* "Man, I'm try'nah do my best, Mr. Upshaw. I made a promise that since my life was spared, I'd try hard to change."

Upshaw nodded his head as if to say he understood. "That's good," he added distantly. "That's great. Now," he continued, turning a page in his folder, "your pre-GED test scores look wonderful. I like that! I talked to your teacher, Mrs. Tucker, and she told me you're a quick learner, but you need to sharpen up more on your math."

Ray sighed. "I know," he interjected. "I've been workin' hard on that. I've got one of my partners, José, who has been tutorin' me."

"That's good." Upshaw continued flipping pages. "Because I asked Mrs. Tucker if she could schedule you for the upcoming GED test. She said she had one coming next month and if she felt you were ready, she would put you on the list."

Ray was confused. He felt like he had missed something. "Why…why did you do that?" he asked out of curiosity.

When he asked this, his probation officer closed the manila folder and talked straight to him. "Turner," he began in one of his most sincere tones. "I locked you up here not because I was being a hard-nosed probation officer, but because I didn't want anything to happen to you."

"What do you mean, you didn't want anything to happen to me?"

"Look, you missed reporting to me a couple of times. Yeah, I was gonna track you down, but you had made it almost a year before almost getting killed. I know kids have trouble being responsible, especially hanging out in those streets. I wanted to find you before this happened to you."

Ray just sat and listened.

"My point is this. You're safe and your mother is safe. That's all I care about."

The look on Ray's face transformed from attentive to confused. He couldn't figure out where Upshaw was going with this conversation. But one thing he knew for sure was that he was all ears.

"I already made it a point to come up here and do a personal visit with you. Then I got a tip from a reliable source last week that informed me that Clayton Branch had been murdered. He took two shots in the head. Now, I know how ya'll operate, but I want you to know that I'm not here to ask you any questions, because there's no need for me to. My source..."

"What do you mean 'your source'?" Ray interjected. "And what does Clayton have to do with me?"

"Whoa, Ray. Now hold on for a minute," Upshaw said sternly. "My source, who is a homicide detective, informed me some months back that an APB had been placed on Clayton Branch, or C-Dog as you call him, for the murder of Macarthur Wilson and Sheila Anderson. They also had one out for the attempted murder of one James Ray Turner, that being you."

Ray couldn't believe that the police were already onto C-Dog. He just listened without saying another word.

Upshaw cleared his throat. "I already knew this. That's why I came to the hospital. Apparently, Branch had been spotted leaving the scene. It wasn't a sure deal until they found him dead last week. The...let's just say he still had the .45 caliber weapon he used to shoot you all with in his possession."

Upshaw's explanation to Ray gave him a whole new outlook on the officer. In his own way, Upshaw was trying to look out for him. But Ray still had questions.

"So, why did you ask my teacher to put me on the list for the GED test next month?"

Upshaw smiled. "Because," he began, leaning back in his chair. "C-Dog's murder changes the whole ballgame. I violated your probation to keep you safe, and now you've made a lot of progress. I came to make you a deal."

A deal? Ray thought. *Here we go.* "A deal like what?"

"If you can show your teacher you're ready and convince her to put you on the list to take the GED, and you pass...I'll put in a recommendation for you to receive an early release. You can be out in a month, no more than a month and a half."

This was music to Ray's ears. "You got a deal!" Ray said with a sense of excitement and purpose.

"Well, you know what you've gotta do." Upshaw stood as a sign that he was finished with their meeting. "Turner, make sure you keep up the good work, and I wish you the best."

"Thanks."

"And ahhh...tell the homie Steele that I'll hit him on the cellie to get the low down on ya' dawg, Fa-shizzole!"

Ray just laughed. Upshaw was burnt-out.

* * *

After the visit with his probation officer, Ray went back and informed everyone of his good news.

First thing's first, he thought. He knew that he had to convince Mrs. Tucker that he was ready. José, Poochie, Joe-Joe, and Buff all told him that they would help him prepare. Ray set his sights on passing his test, and he used Momma Wilson, Trena, and his freedom as his motivation.

For the next few weeks he studied, and he studied hard. His weakness was math. José knew a young Asian guy who was a math guru, and he and José double-teamed Ray to get him ready. Day after day he did his best to understand the formulas to solve algebra problems.

During the process of his studies, Ray went regularly to his medical appointments. During these visits, his therapist informed him that Doctor Brooks said he was ready to remove Ray from wheelchair status. What he didn't know was that Ray had taken Buff up on his offer, and every night for an hour he had begun doing a light workout to get his strength back. He was glad, too, because it had helped him out a lot.

*   *   *

"Oh my good God Almighty!"

When Ray went to visit that week and only Momma Wilson showed up, she saw him standing on his own.

"God surely is good," she said with tears in her eyes. "Look at my son. You look so handsome. I wish Trena could see you right now."

Ray was all smiles. "Thanks, Momma," he said bashfully. "You know, Upshaw came up here and told me that if I pass my GED, he'll make a recommendation to the judge for me to get an early release."

Momma Wilson shook her head in amazement. "Baby, he did?"

"Yeah, and he said that the police already knew that C-Dog shot us." Ray hesitated. "He said they were lookin' for him up until the day that he was found dead, too."

Mrs. Wilson clasped her hands together and positioned them on her chin in a praying position. She had wrinkles in her lips as she shook her head. "God is good, baby."

Ray nodded in agreement. "Momma, it's funny how things come back on people when they least expect it."

Momma Wilson was still shaking her head. "Baby, God has a way of giving justice. He also has a way of showing mercy to those that He chooses. God seen it all and He had mercy on your life," she said with emphasis.

Yeah, what's done in the dark will always come to light, Ray thought.

Momma Wilson continued. "Speaking of God, you know who I saw at Bible study last Wednesday?"

Curious, Ray asked, "Who, Momma?"

Mrs. Wilson smiled. "Ketta! Do you remember Ketta?"

Ray looked lost. "Ketta..." he mumbled in a distant tone.

"Baby, remember...she was a schoolteacher and..."

"Oh," Ray interjected, as if his memory had been jarred. "Yeah, yeah," he said as he reflected on the last time he'd seen her and she had asked him for a twenty-dollar rock of cocaine. He smiled, remembering the bet he'd made with her, and the last words she uttered about going to church. "What's up with her?"

"Well, Wednesday night at church she told me to tell you something about you guys were even, or something like that."

"Ketta was at church?" Ray asked in a disbelieving tone.

"Yeah, baby, and she said she's been clean for six months now. She even had her kids with her. Baby, she looked good, too."

Ray smiled. *I guess she's through with that stuff,* he thought.

*　*　*

Counselor Steele had just finished working a full shift at the facility and was extremely tired. His dedication to his work pushed him over the edge sometimes, but he never allowed it to drag him down. Now, as he walked through the parking lot toward his 2010 Dodge Ram pickup truck, Steele was stirred out of his exhausted state by the ring of his cell phone.

"Hello," he answered, opening the driver's side of his vehicle.

"Hello, William is this you?" a voice asked.

"Yes, it is," he replied. "May I ask who this is?"

The person on the other end of the line seemed to be busy doing something. Steele could hear pages being ruffled around.

"Will, this is Tom."

Steele gave off a slight chuckle. "Tom, you sounded real professional. You almost made me think you were a bill collector or someone. What's goin' on? I was expectin' your call."

The caller laughed. "Yeah, I'm in the office right now so I have to be, you know?"

"I hear you, Upshaw," Steele said with a chuckle of his own.

Steele and Upshaw went back many years. To Steele it was sort of weird how their paths seemed to cross after all this time. Upshaw was upbeat, like always.

"Man, I would've called you sooner but I've been real busy, you know?"

"Yeah, man, I just got off and you can bet I'm dirt tired," Steele admitted as he climbed into the truck, resting in its comfortable interior.

"I've been swamped with a heavy case load," Upshaw continued, "and one in particular has me really concerned."

Steele sighed. "Let me guess, Turner?"

"Exactly!"

Steele leaned back against the headrest and said, "Good kid, reminds me of us back in our day. There's somethin' about him that makes me wanna believe he has a chance."

"I agree, because I feel the same way. I've been dealin' with him for two years now and I can't seem to give up on him, or any of these young kids out here, for that matter."

That's exactly what Steele appreciated about Upshaw. He was someone who really wanted to help the youths. "Well, we can't give up, can we? If we do that then they'll never be able to find the answers they're lookin' for."

Upshaw agreed again. "Will, you know I've been out here with you for ten years now, trying to come up with a solution to help these kids. I see the hurdles they face in life coming out of those communities, but I don't want them to use those obstacles as an excuse for the choices they make in life. I just want to help."

"Tom, you've already helped by just bein' there like you've been," Steele encouraged after a pause. "See, I'm from those streets. And everybody that comes out of these communities doesn't sell drugs, rob, or gangbang. You have maybe one percent who choose this lifestyle. So, there's no excuse, and you're doin' good."

"But it doesn't seem like it's enough, because for a long time I was a part of the problem, as well."

"Yeah, you were affiliated with the California Aryan Brothers at one time, and maybe you did a lot of things that you're not proud of. But you can't let a guilty conscience be the reason that you're fightin' for those kids out there. When Turner told me you were goin' to call me, I knew somethin' was botherin' you."

"Will, it's not just my past affiliations, or even a guilty conscience," Upshaw insisted with a slight pause. "But gangs in the United States have grown to over one million members, responsible for over eighty percent of the crimes in communities across the nation. I just read a report that said almost a million gang members live within inner city communities, and over 140,000 are in jail. This is what bothers me when I go out into these communities. All I see are more potential slaves to this gang and drug defeated mentality."

Steele paused, contemplating his thoughts. "I

remember when I first met you in Corcoran some twelve years ago on the Four Yard. You didn't want anything to do with my kind. I was a Bible toting ex-gang member who was on a mission to try to save the world," he said, laughing. "But, against all odds, you changed. You changed even though you knew covering up your A.B. patch was like committing suicide. You knew you couldn't walk another prison yard ever again in life because the A.B.s would kill you."

Upshaw cleared his throat. "Yeah, I changed. But Will, it was easy for me because I wasn't reared to hate people. See, I was caught up in prison politics, following people who believed that every race was unclean except the White race. But this wasn't me. I don't believe we should dislike a person because of the color of their skin. But these kids…these kids are out there selling drugs and hurting each other just to be able to represent the color of a bandanna or hat."

Steele exhaled heavily. "Tom," he began in a calm voice. "Most of these kids aren't raised like that, either. This mentality usually starts outside the home. See, it doesn't matter if it's the color of a person's skin, bandanna, or hat, the point is we changed that mentality."

"Yeah, I guess you're right," Upshaw agreed softly.

"You changed even though you didn't become a part of the Christian community. You found a way out of that gang stuff even when your life was at risk." Steele paused again. "Now look at you. You've sacrificed your life for what you believe in now, and I know if you can just save one of those kids, it's worth it."

Officer Upshaw was silent as he listened to Counselor Steele. But something just wouldn't let him hold his peace. "Will," he stuttered. "I know saving one is better than saving none but…in my area of San Bernardino County alone there are over three hundred and sixty gangs. And over twelve thousand gang members! Not to mention

Riverside County just gave five million to its Sheriff's department's budget to form a county wide gang task force. I mean, is saving one kid really enough?"

Steele hesitated, contemplating Upshaw's thoughts. "Yes, but whether one or all, we have to reeducate them just like we were reeducated. A lot of them came from the Los Angeles area just like I did. Concerned parents moved their families from Los Angeles to the Greater Riverside and Inland Empire areas in hopes to escape the gang threats there, and to find cheaper housing. However, most children are so immersed in the gang lifestyle that by the time they turn twelve years old it's already too late, and they end up spreading gangs and their criminal behavior into their new communities. So, I believe it's our duty to become mentors and educate them if we can."

"It's funny you say that," Upshaw commented. "You know, it's cheaper to educate our youths rather than throwing them away for the rest of their lives. As far back as 2002, a study revealed that every one dollar spent on juvenile detention centers to lock these kids up returned almost two dollars in terms of reduced crime and cost of crime to taxpayers."

"Is that right?"

"Man, they saved somewhere between three and thirteen dollars for a series of detention alternatives like Project Bridge, which is a anti-gang program. Not to mention all of the programs out there for Diversion, Aggressive Replacement Training, and mentorships that bring these kids to various prisons to talk to inmates who try to encourage them in the direction for change before it's too late."

"Yeah, you're right about that alternative stuff," Steele agreed. "They also have a lot of organizations who offer faith-based initiatives that help and assist at-risk youths."

"Will, I know there's a more effective way to reduce

youth offending. I'm not worried about job security like some people who work for the Department of Corrections and the Juvenile Justice System. I just don't want Turner — or any of these kids, for that matter — to feel as though they're a lost cause."

"Tom, they're not a lost cause. And caring about someone's life is more important than any job security," Steele interjected. "All we gotta do is continue to be there for them like we've been."

Upshaw agreed. "You know, that's the reason for my call. That kid Turner — there's something special about him. He has a chance because he's still breathing, and I know his story. His mother was murdered when he was seven years old, and he has never met his father. He was reared by a family that loves him. And it just so happens that one of the people who reared him was one of his mother's suppliers at the time. I guess that's why my heart goes out to him, and I just want you to stay on top of him. Don't let him give up on himself."

"Tom, I got him. Don't worry."

Chapter Twenty

The time had come. Out of the blue José pulled Ray to the side and told him that he was going home in a week. Ray was happy for his friend, and thankful for all the help he had given him.

"I should be ready," Ray said. "Mrs. Tucker told me yesterday that she felt I was ready to take my test. She's gonna put me on the list to take it next week."

Both Ray and José realized that Ray was going to take the test the same day that José was going home.

* * *

"Man, pass me another one of those burritos," Joe-Joe hollered through a mouth filled with food.

Buff laughed at how stuffed Joe-Joe's jaws were with food. "Fat boy, you need to slow down," he told him. "That's like your twelfth one."

Poochie rolled him another burrito and said, "Don't tell him nothin', Buff, let him bust!"

Joe-Joe squirmed in his seat. "I'm not gonna bust. I got this thang under control."

Ray, Buff, Joe-Joe, José, and Poochie all sat around eating and drinking sodas together. They were celebrating José's last night with them.

"Yo', José," Poochie began. "You want another one?"

José smiled, nodding his head. "Yeah, bring it on!"

"I don't see ya'll clownin' my burritos now," Poochie said with a proud look on his face.

Ray laughed and gave Poochie a slight waving gesture, appearing to brush off his comment. "Naw man, the burritos are the bomb."

His comment brought a bigger smile to Poochie's

face.

José turned to Ray, trying to swallow the food that was in his mouth before he spoke. "Your P.O. is gonna see that you passed your test, and he's gonna let you go."

Ray smiled with his jaws full of food. "I hope so," he mumbled.

"Man, you studied hard. I wish I could stay to see you pass."

"Don't trip, José. I'll be out there with you in a minute. You'll have my hookup and my P.O.'s hookup before you leave," Ray assured him.

Just then Javier and a few of his homeboys walked up. "Hey, José," Javier began, without any expression on his face. "Can I talk to you for a minute?"

José looked around at the guys he sat eating with. "Yeah," he replied. "You can holler at me right here. They're cool."

Javier nodded his head and said, "Right on, holmes. I just wanted to apologize to you for the way we acted before. That was wrong and you were right. I know your people, homeboy. Your mom and sisters have always been nice to me. I hope you go out there and do good, *esse*, for reals!"

José was moved. Javier and his partners were serious and the looks on their faces said so. "Thanks, holmes, I appreciate that."

Ray and his buddies were sitting around watching the discussion when Poochie jumped up out of nowhere. "So, what's up, ya'll wanna try one of my famous burritos?"

Javier and his buddies looked at each other. At first Ray thought they would view it as disrespecting some type of code. He knew that the South Siders and Tiny Dukes had a code that they lived by: Never take food that's been opened from another race. Ray sat and shook his head, anticipating his response. For that split second it seemed as though time stood still.

Javier looked at Poochie and smiled. "Why not, holmes? They look good."

Ray exhaled with relief.

"Yeah," Javier's partners said with enthusiasm.

"Come on, ya'll," Poochie added with excitement in his voice. "This is José's last day."

Chapter Twenty-One

"Man, you take care," poured out of Ray's mouth with much emotion and respect for his newfound friend. "Make sure you..."

"Look," José interrupted. "I know how to contact you. I got your mom's and probation officer's hookups. You just make sure you do well on the test so we can get together soon."

Ray laughed at his friends seriousness. "All right man, I will."

The two friends then shook hands and embraced. Ray stood and watched as José made his way out of the building. He had given Ray a lot of inspiration, and Ray was determined to make sure he used it for the test he would take later that day.

"Hey, Turner!"

It was Counselor Steele calling from his office. Ray turned around and smiled at the sight of Counselor Steele standing in his doorway dressed in blue uniformed khaki shorts, black boots, and a pair of tube socks pulled up to his knees. With a soft laugh, he nodded his head in acknowledgement that he had heard him as he made his way to his office.

"What's up Steele?"

Steele smiled. "So, today's the big day?"

Ray shrugged. "Yeah, but I'm nervous though."

Counselor Steele sat in his chair and leaned back. "Come in and have a seat."

Ray looked around. "Do you want me to close the door?"

"Naw, you can leave it open." Steele sat and looked at Ray for a moment. "Have you ever read the story about David and Goliath?"

Ray looked at Counselor Steele, wondering where

he was going with this conversation. "Yeah, yeah, I've read it before. It's about a young dude who beat down a big dude named Goliath."

Steele laughed, placing his hand over his mouth to conceal it. "Boy, is that all you remember from the story? You didn't get anything else from it?"

Ray thought, and then said, "Basically, it don't matter how big you are or how big you think you are, anybody can get punished when they're slippin'."

Counselor Steele laughed again at Ray's assessment of the story, then shook his head. "You're absolutely right, Turner. Anybody can get punished. But the story...the story has somethin' else to offer you. It has a deeper meanin' that you can use and apply to every aspect of your life. It's a meanin' that can help to encourage you when you're feelin' doubtful."

Ray sat and stared at Steele. He didn't know what he was talking about. "Like what?"

"See, everyone has a giant in their life to destroy." Steele hesitated, looking at Ray. "One of the biggest giants that exists for most people is called fear."

Fear! Ray thought.

"This is the Goliath that hinders most people from doin' or becomin' certain things in life. I talk to a lot of young people like you who want to get out of gangs, but they're afraid of the possible repercussions, or what their so-called homeboys might think about them. They're afraid that they won't be accepted anymore. So, they hold onto the known instead of embracin' the unknown. Then you have Goliath's brothers — racism, hatred, envy, jealousy, and anger — which promote the giant's cause. And for some of us, our Goliath is simply the fear that if we stop sellin' drugs or robbin' people, we won't have any other way to make enough money to have a nice home, because we don't know anything else. But fear kills because some of us don't make it out of the gangs or streets alive."

Ray interjected, "But a lot of us don't have any other way to make money or survive."

"Turner..." Steele shook his head. "There's always goin' to be a way to make an honest livin' without sellin' drugs or havin' to rob someone who's worked their entire life to get what they have. And you will always have the choice in life to make a decision, if you don't wait until it's too late. But because of fear of steppin' out of that lifestyle to try somethin' new, you've made yourself believe that there's no other way."

Ray interrupted with a sigh. "It ain't, Steele, I'm tellin' you!"

Steele shook his head and stared at Ray with a serious look in his eyes. "Turner, just listen. I used to be gang-affiliated, sold drugs, and would rob somethin' if I caught someone slippin'. But look at me now. I had to make a choice how I wanted to live the rest of my life, and when I did, I stood on it. You have to do the same thing in your life. You have to become David and destroy your Goliath. You have to take on these challenges that life has to offer you. Stop worryin' about failure and just believe in everything you do. Startin' with this test today."

Ray nodded as if to say he understood.

Steele leaned forward, resting his forearms on his desk. "When you walk into that room with Mrs. Tucker, know that you have the same spirit as David. Behead your giant and just believe every time you mark an answer down that it's right. Just believe within yourself, son."

When Counselor Steele finished talking, Ray nodded his head with confidence in his eyes. He smiled.

"I see you nodded, but do you really understand what I'm sayin' to you?" Steele asked him.

Ray nodded again. "Yeah, I got you. Goliath's dead, so ain't no use of me bein' scared of failin' because I'mma pass my test," Ray expressed with confidence.

Counselor Steele picked up a file off his desk.

"Now, get out of here and get ready to take your test. I have some work to do."

*   *   *

"You can begin your test...now!" Mrs. Tucker said as she pushed the button on her hand-held stopwatch.

Ray took a deep breath and then thought, *Goliath you're goin' down!*

The test was broken up into many sections, and each had its rough spots for Ray. He occasionally looked around to see if he was the only one having problems, and quickly realized that he wasn't. As time ran out, he started to get discouraged, thinking that he had already missed too many questions. But he didn't let that cause him to quit. He pushed forward.

Finally, he watched as Mrs. Tucker stood up from her desk and stretched. "Okay, gentlemen, pencils down."

Ray looked at the clock. Two and a half hours had passed. He had been given various booklets with questions, and now it was all over. *I hope I did good*, he thought. *I gave it my all.*

After the students were finished with their tests, they were released for the remainder of the day. Ray went back to his housing unit, feeling like he had just stepped out of the boxing ring with Mike Tyson. He was beat. And when he reached the unit, Poochie, Buff, and Joe-Joe were waiting on him.

"Here you go, dawg."

Buff handed Ray a small note that was folded up like a paper triangle. "José told me to give this to you when you finished takin' your test."

Ray took the note and headed toward his bunk, his three friends trailing him.

"What it say, Ray?" Joe-Joe inquired.

Ray sat down on his bunk and opened the letter and

began to read it.

Dear Ray,
I hate that I can't be there after you finish your test. But I know that you passed, don't worry. What I really wanted to tell you is when you come home, don't be scared to try something new, because you can't keep living that same lifestyle and expect to get different results. Ain't no love in those streets! Be like Peter, Ray, and step out of that place and walk on water. Do you remember what water is symbolic of? I know you do. Don't worry about the storm. Just like you stayed focused for the test, keep your eyes on whatever you want to do and I promise you, you won't sink. I'll be here for you when you come home. Family before gangs.
Brothers in Christ,
José

The letter was encouraging and Ray found that his doubts about the test were gone. "Come on ya'll," Ray said to his friends. "Let's play some spades."

"Spades!" Poochie exclaimed. "What'chu know about spades?"

Ray looked at him and said, "We about to find out. Me and Joe-Joe will play you and bumb...I mean Buff."

Poochie and Buff laughed at Ray's play of humor.

Joe-Joe looked at Ray and said, "You better not be heavy like a bump truck, because I can't carry no extra weight."

Ray laughed, because he knew that it was coming.

"Boy," Poochie interjected humorously, "you already carryin' extra weight, fat boy!"

Chapter Twenty-Two

Ray was nervous. Poochie kept telling him to be cool, but he couldn't help it. Buff told him he had nothing to worry about, but it didn't feel like it. He was bubbling with anticipation and fear.

"Mail call!" the unit officer yelled.

Ray knew it was on its way because his teacher told him to look for it. Now, waiting in the cluster of young men, Ray held his breath until he heard his name.

"Turner!" someone yelled.

Ray looked up and over the heads of the others, but was confused. The officer handing out the mail wasn't who was calling his name.

"Turner!" the voice yelled out again.

Ray turned to see that it was Counselor Steele calling him. The look on Counselor Steele's face was serious. "Turner, let me talk to you for a second."

"Sandoval...Fields...Beard...Camron...Winrow..." the officer was calling and handing out the mail.

"Yo', Turner, let me holla' at'chu," Steele said again, but Ray was torn between getting his mail and seeing what in the world his counselor wanted. "Man, let me holla' at'chu, Turner."

Ray was hesitant. He couldn't take it anymore. "Man, Steele, hold up for a minute!" he exclaimed, noticing that Steele had a grin on his face.

"Man, you actin' like you waitin' on somethin'!"

Ray cut his eyes in Counselor Steele's direction. "You know I'm lookin' for my GED results and..."

Steele shook his head, still smiling.

"Turner!"

Ray turned toward the officer calling his name and said, "Yeah, right here!"

Poochie, Joe-Joe, and Buff were standing next to

him in anticipation, as if they were waiting on their own test results. Ray retrieved the folded piece of paper from the officer. It was sealed with a staple, and he held it without looking at its results.

"You want me to open it for you, Ray?" Poochie asked.

"Naw," he answered, staring at the paper in his hand. He couldn't move. He just stood until finally he looked up and saw Counselor Steele standing to his side looking at him. "Aye, yo', Steele," he said looking up at him.

"What's up, Turner?"

"Would you open this for me?"

Counselor Steele smiled and shrugged his shoulders. "Sure."

Ray handed him the paper and the man said, "I'm going to take it in here and open it up after I make this call..." and he walked away.

Ray was hot on his tracks. "Come on, Steele, don't do me like that!"

Still holding the paper with the results in his hand, Steele smiled even bigger. "What do you mean? Where's your faith?"

Ray placed both hands over his ears and shook his head. "What? Come on, man. Not right now."

"What do you mean not right now? Where's your faith? You don't believe you passed?"

"That's what I'm try'nah see!"

"Did you do your best?"

Ray eyed him with impatience. "Man, you know I did."

"Is your stuff packed?"

Ray looked confused. "No."

"And, why not?"

Ray was frustrated at this point and didn't feel like going through any of this. "Why would I need to do that? I need to pass first."

Steele looked at him, and shook his head. "You know that you received this in the mail today, but the results came back a week ago. Your probation officer could've already called and gotten the results, put you in for your early release, and been on his way up here by now. So, I'm askin' you. Where's your faith? Don't you remember what I told you about David and Goliath?"

Ray shrugged. "Yeah, but..."

Steele shook his head again and exhaled. He saw that Ray still didn't get it. He tossed the paper on his desk. "Open it."

Ray took the paper and popped the staple. He unfolded it and read the results. When he raised his eyes Counselor Steele was looking directly at him.

"You passed by one point, Turner," he said, smiling at Ray. "Go pack your stuff. Your P.O. is on the way as we speak. You're goin' home today."

Ray couldn't believe his ears. He was going home! "Man, Steele, you ain't..."

Steele smiled. "I wouldn't play with you like that. I'm serious, you probably only have about a half an hour at most."

Hearing that he was about to be released, Ray spun on his heels and headed for the office door, only to stop in its midst. He slowly turned back around, displaying a half of a smile.

"Turner, what's wrong?" Steele inquired curiously.

Ray's face now turned serious. "You asked me somethin' a while back and I just wanted to let you know that I figured out what I really wanna do with my life."

Steele paused, then smiled. "And?"

"Well, I was lookin' at this show on TV a few nights ago where they were solvin' old murder cases and it made me think about my mom, and how they never found the person who killed her."

"You mean cold cases?"

Ray shrugged. "Yeah, I think that's it. But it made me wonder after that about how many people like me have someone they love that's been killed and nobody has found the person who did it."

Counselor Steele just listened attentively.

"I mean I know my mom was on the streets sellin' herself and strung out on drugs but..." Ray hesitated for a few seconds, then cleared his throat. "But she was still my mom and I loved her. People don't care about people like us from the 'hood because we can't afford to pay people to find out the truth when somethin' goes wrong with us. But that was my mom, regardless of what she was doin'." Ray wiped the corner of his eye to catch a tear. "I wanna become one of those people who solves old cases. I wanna find out who killed my mom."

Counselor Steele was stunned and lost for words. He hadn't expected this from Ray, but he embraced the conversation. "You mean a forensic specialist," Steele smiled. "Son, you can become anybody you want to be when you put your mind into it. And the person that did that to your mom, you'll find him."

Ray smiled, drying his eyes. *Yeah*, he thought as he turned and left the office. As he made his way back to the housing unit, everyone wanted to know the results.

"I passed!" he exclaimed, throwing his hands in the air like a championship fighter. "My P.O. is on his way to get me."

"Right now?" exclaimed Poochie.

"Yep!"

Buff heard everything he needed to hear. "Well, let's get'chu packed."

Ray looked at him and said, "Man, that's the easy part." Ray patted his back pocket to make sure he had his small pocket Bible with him. He went to his bunk and grabbed two more things: his letters and the leather-bound

Bible José left him. "I'm ready." Ray sat around and joked with his friends for a little while before he had to leave. "Man, you and Joe-Joe better look out for each other."

"Man, L'il Ray, you know we gonna do that. We homeboys," Poochie said proudly.

"Naw, man, ya'll are friends," Ray corrected him.

Time went so fast, and before long Ray got the call he had been waiting for. Counselor Steele personally yelled his name and came to escort him outside. Ray said his goodbyes and left the building.

No more D-Unit!

As Ray departed the building, Counselor Steele walked with him to the parking lot with his hand around his shoulder. Immediately he noticed something that caught his eye. A Black Raven 2009 Cadillac STS with tinted windows sat in the parking lot. It had 22" Lion Heart rims on it. Ray knew that car anywhere. It was Big Mack's. The scene was like déjà vu. Butterflies filled his stomach as he relived the last few moments he had shared with Big Mack, and it did something weird to him. But then he noticed as the car doors opened it was Momma Wilson who exited on the driver's side, and Trena stepped out of the passenger's side. Ray smiled and ran over to them.

"Momma," he cried out as he noticed Trena's radiant smile.

"Baby, they just released his car from being impounded. The police had it during their investigation," Momma Wilson explained. "But, baby, it's too much for me, and I believe Macarthur would want you to have it anyways."

Just as Ray gave her a big hug, the passenger's door opened again and out jumped his probation officer, Upshaw. "We big rollin' up in this thang, dawg! Rollin' on 22s."

Trena looked at Ray, who just shrugged his shoulders as they began to laugh.

"You did good, Turner, and I'm proud of you. You kept your end of the bargain, so you know ya' boy gotta keep it real, fa-show."

Ray laughed. "Oh yeah?"

"Oh yeah," Upshaw said, imitating him. "And before I forget, some guy named José called and said he had a job waiting on you. Something about building houses or something? Turner, you already took, what, three, four, five like ya' boy Tupac, behind something you shouldn't have been involved in from the beginning. I hope the only bricks you're going to be handling are the one that don't get people high."

Ray shook his head. "Man, Upshaw, I'm done with all that. José got me a job and I'mma pay my way through school to become a forensic specialist," he said with a smile.

Upshaw smiled as he looked at Momma Wilson. "You're gonna make us all proud of you, son."

"Yeah," Ray said, nodding his head. "José, family is more important than a gang," he whispered.

~ THE END ~

Note from the Author

Even though Nelles was only a stage for this story, the reality of these events is real, especially when our kids have been shot, stabbed, robbed, or even worse, have been killed on each and every one of our street corners due to gang and/or drug related violence. Most, if not all teens who grow up in these poverty-stricken environments are influenced by other people's actions, led into believing that drugs and gangs are cool, or are the only solution to raising themselves from the bottomless pit they see themselves in. They gravitate toward individuals looking for some kind of hope, or something to sustain them. And others follow these individuals because of Goliath (fears), especially when many male family figures are, or have been, incarcerated. This is a sad truth because this cycle continues to exist.

For example, if you are the type who watches the news or reads the newspaper, then you are aware of the growing problem that exists with our youth. Through the juvenile courts and the adult Criminal Justice System, the United States incarcerates more of our youths than any other country in the world, a reflection of the larger trends in incarceration practices in the United States. In 2002, approximately 126,000 juveniles were incarcerated in youth detention facilities alone. Approximately 500,000 youths are brought to detention centers in a given year. Sad to say, there are between 60,000 and 80,000 female gang members in the U.S. Approximately 32,000 of these members are teenagers, and 48,000 are adults. And, out of these staggering numbers, approximately 14,000 of these teen girls are held in correctional and residential facilities. The sad part of this staggering number is that the majority of the 14,000 girls have some gang affiliation, even though how many is actually unclear.

A recent CNN report stated that the U.S. has approximately 2,500 youths serving life sentences. And, in *USA Today*, an article on Monday, November 9, 2009 revealed that there are 111 young offenders in the U.S. who have no possibility of parole for nonlethal crimes. These numbers are mind-boggling, especially when a recent report on youth incarceration revealed that incarcerating youths can aggravate mental illness.

According to detention center administrators who testified to the United States Congress in a 2004 Special Investigation by the House of Representatives, many incarcerated youths could have avoided incarceration had they received mental health treatment. This report further found that detention centers do not promote normal cognitive and emotional development. The report indicated that for up to one-third of incarcerated youths suffering from depression, the onset of depression occurred after their transfer to a detention center. These youths face a greater risk of self-injury and suicide. Researchers have found that incarcerated youths engage in self-injurious behavior at a rate two to four times higher than any other incarcerated population. Furthermore, prison administrative policy often intensifies the risk by responding to suicidal threats in ways that endanger the detainees, such as putting them in solitary confinement.

Studies indicate that incarcerating young offenders is not the most effective way of curbing delinquency and reducing crime. The relationship between detention of young offenders and the rate of overall youth criminality is not evident. But, a study of the Federal Bureau of Investigation's arrest data for the 1990s revealed that the rise in detention was unrelated to crime rates. That is, detention as a tactic of controlling young offenders has little to nothing to do with the rate of crime or the "threat" that youths pose to the public.

While there may be an individual need to incarcerate violent, high-risk youths, most of the young people in prisons, jails, and detention centers today — up to 70 percent — are serving time for nonviolent offenses. It is a proven fact that as many as one-third of all Americans might engage in delinquent behavior at some point in their youth. But those that are detained or imprisoned are less likely to grow out of their delinquency than those that are not. Criminologists recognized a natural process of desistance called "aging out" of delinquency, through which a person desists their delinquent behavior through maturation and experience. Detaining or incarcerating youth can interrupt or slow down the aging out process, resulting in a longer period of delinquency.

Most activists in the movement to end youth incarceration believe that the best way to mitigate the impact of detention and incarceration on our youths is to reduce the number of youths that pass through the system. By improving credible alternatives to incarceration, this portion of the movement provides opportunities for communities to treat, rather than punish, young offenders, much the way the juvenile justice system was founded to do.

It is evident that there is growing drug and gang related violence in the United States, and particularly in most Southern and Midwest states like Illinois, Texas, and states like Maryland. The only way to save our youths is by reeducating them. All it takes is one individual at a time to step forward and accept the baton of faith — an unwavering faith that believes every one of our kids in the United States has more good in them than bad; a faith that believes even though the good and the bad is within each and every one of us, God is able to separate the wheat from the tare and make our kids productive members in society.

Each and every one of us has the Spirit of Counselor Steele, Officer Upshaw, and/or Little Ray...if we're willing to step up and accept the baton, and start trying to help change and save our younger generation. Just like José's dad taught him that family is more important than a gang, this principle holds true about the family of the United States. We are a race, the human race, and what affects one affects the other. Whether we realize it or not, we are connected. This effort to save and reeducate starts right here and right now! We can't afford to just turn a blind eye and continue to leave it up to the Criminal Justice System to throw away our youth without the belief that each and every one of them can be rehabilitated. It takes us, the people, our communities, and each and every community leader of all organizations to intervene. It doesn't matter if you're the one who wants to change, or the one who's willing to help someone else make a change, our younger generation is the key ingredient to building a healthy and productive future, and Lord knows we need them.

Let's help to save and reeducate our youth. By helping to save and reeducate them, we will play a major role in saving our environment. They are the future, and they are the ones who will become caretakers over the environment that we are to live in. I know...because I am a product of it.

— A.J. Scott

Resources:

http://library.sprc.org/item.php?id=332&catid=19. Prepared for Sen. Susan Collins and Rep. Henry A. Waxman

Kashani, J.H.; Manning, G.W.; McKnew, D.H.; Cytrn, L.; Simonds, J.F. and Wooderson, P.C. (1980) "Depression Among Incarcerated Delinquents," Psychiatry Resources Vol. 1 p. 185-191

Parent, D.G. Leiter, V.; Kennedy, S.; Livens, L.; Wentworth, D. & Wilcox, S. (1994) Conditions of Confinement: Juvenile Detention and Corrections Facilities. Washington, DC: U.S. Department of Justice, Office of Juvenile Justice and Delinquency Prevention

Hayes, L.M. (1999) Suicide Prevention in Juvenile Correctional Facilities. Washington, DC: Department of Justice, Office of Juvenile Justice and Delinquency Prevention

Sickmund, M. (2007). Juveniles in Corrections - Washington DC: Office of Juvenile Justice and Delinquency Prevention

Sickmund, M.; Sladky, T.J.; Kang, W. (2004). "Census of Juveniles in Residential Placement Databook." http://www.ojjdp.ncjrs.org/ojstatbb/cjrp. Retrieved 2009-11-06
http://en.wikipedia.org/wiki/Youth_incarceration_in_the_United_States

About the Author

A.J. Scott was born and raised in Southern California. He is an accused gang associate and former drug dealer, presently serving a federal life sentence for conspiracy to distribute cocaine.

He is the proud father of three: Dante, Amesha, and Amos Jr., II. However, since his incarceration in 2000, he has rededicated his life to Christ. He is presently working toward his Master's Degree in Theology through Channel Island Bible College & Seminary. He has earned his Credentials of Ministry and his credentials as a Christian Counselor from Channel Island Bible College & Seminary. He has earned his diploma as a Paralegal and Legal Assistant from Blackstone Career Institute. Mr. Scott has been certified through the Foundation for a Drug-Free World as a Drug Prevention Specialist.

In his spare time, Mr. Scott teaches legal writing and is a Suicide Companion to fellow inmates experiencing the difficulties that come with incarceration. His next project is to become a mentor to at-risk youths. He is a lover of life and believes that God has a divine purpose for each and every one of our lives.

~ Portions of the proceeds will be donated to help at-risk youths. ~